THE PASSAGEWAY WAS

"Ahh! Ahh!" Doreen █████████████ another to avoid a mass of █████████████ low, and black ████ kes. She was terrified and fell into Larry █████

"Okay, d█████ ████ ████ ████ slung Doreen's arm over his ███████ ██ ██████ her stumble forward. He started into the next tunnel and stopped dead. "I hope there's another way back."

"Me too." Paige shone her flashlight inside the narrow stone corridor. The passage floor was covered with snakes. Several began shedding their skins.

"Cross-country," Tammy said, taking charge. Ignoring the snakes sliding out of the rock pile, she climbed it. "This way."

Paige let Joyce and Daniel go first, then steadied Larry as he carried Doreen up the rock pile. When Paige reached the top, she realized that cutting through the woods was only a slightly better alternative than taking the tunnels.

The ground was alive with thousands of writhing snakes.

Charmed®

Published by Simon & Schuster

MYSTIC KNOLL

An original novel by Diana G. Gallagher

Based on the hit TV series created by

Constance M. Burge

SIMON SPOTLIGHT ENTERTAINMENT
New York   London   Toronto   Sydney

This book is a work of fiction. Any references to historical events, real people, or real locales are used fictitiously. Other names, characters, places, and incidents are the product of the author's imagination, and any resemblance to actual events or locales or persons, living or dead, is entirely coincidental.

S|S|E

SIMON SPOTLIGHT ENTERTAINMENT
An imprint of Simon & Schuster Children's Publishing Division
1230 Avenue of the Americas, New York, New York 10020
® & © 2005 Spelling Television Inc. All Rights Reserved.
All rights reserved, including the right of reproduction in whole or in part in any form.
SIMON SPOTLIGHT ENTERTAINMENT and related logo are trademarks of Simon & Schuster, Inc.
Manufactured in the United States of America
First Edition 10 9 8 7 6 5 4 3 2 1
Library of Congress Control Number 2004108435
ISBN 0-689-86854-5

For my sister, Wendy—
Thanks for the New Hampshire vacations
And the salt & pepper frogs!

Chapter

1

With a basket of fresh gardenia blooms in one hand and a cup of herbal tea in the other, Paige paused at the living-room door on her way back to the attic. Leaning against the doorjamb, she watched supermom Piper in action.

"'Whee!'" Piper exclaimed, reading from a children's picture book. She sat on the sofa with baby Wyatt propped up beside her. "'Puddles are *fun!*'"

"Eeee!" Wyatt squealed.

"'Big paws make *big* splashes.' See?" Piper pointed to the picture in the book.

Paige laughed. Wyatt turned to look at his aunt and squealed again.

Piper looked up at her sister with a smile. "Welcome to the distract-baby-so-he-doesn't-use-his-powers story hour."

"Whatever works," Paige said. They couldn't

be sure what might trigger Wyatt's developing imagination, but they weren't taking any chances. A week ago he had turned his plastic bathtub toys into real turtles and ducks. He wouldn't change them back until the ducks escaped and started to fly away.

"What are you reading?" Paige asked.

"*Good Dog, Bad Dog.*" Piper held up the book. The cover pictured a large white dog with floppy ears, a red tongue, and big black spots.

"Sounds fascinating for a toddler tome," Paige said. "But isn't Wyatt too young to understand it?"

"Probably, but I figure it can't hurt to start teaching him right from wrong." Piper brushed Wyatt's hair with her hand. "I've been doing some research on how young kids learn. Reading aloud imprints words and, eventually, the relevant concepts in little baby brains."

"Well, good luck with that," Paige said. "I'm off to practice potions."

"Anything in particular?" Piper asked, eyeing the basket of flowers and inhaling the pungent scent. "Gardenias. Are you stressed?"

Yes! Paige thought, exasperated. *Because I've been working nights and weekends at extra temp jobs to save money for a vacation nobody wants to take!*

"More tired than strung out," she explained. She didn't want to start an argument, but she had to be honest. "And since I can't convince you or Phoebe to get away from it all for a couple of weeks, which we all desperately need to do, I'll have to settle for herbal tea and the soothing properties of fresh flowers."

"We're the Charmed Ones," Piper said. "We can never get away from it all."

Paige rolled her eyes. "You know what I mean."

"Yes, and you know the magical mission is just one reason we're a no-go for vacation." Piper sighed. "I can't leave P3 for two weeks, Paige. There's payroll and ordering—"

"Isn't that why you hired a manager?" Paige interrupted. "To take care of things so you can spend more time at home with your family?"

"At *home*," Piper repeated, "where I'm only a few minutes away from P3 if anything goes wrong."

"Except you haven't had to rush off to handle a single emergency since the guy started two months ago," Paige countered.

Piper wasn't swayed. "We can't afford to go on vacation."

"If you ask me, we can't afford not to," Paige muttered.

"Buh!" Wyatt pounded the book with his small hand.

"Let's talk about this later, okay?" Piper lowered the book so Wyatt could see the pictures. "Look, Wyatt! 'Puppy puddles!'"

Paige trudged up the stairs. Between the extra temp jobs and the inescapable demands of being one of the three most powerful witches in the world, she was more exhausted than she had admitted. Being overtired had diminished her mental acuity and physical readiness, which endangered all of them.

No wonder I'm stressed out, Paige thought as she entered the attic. She set the basket of gardenias and the cup of tea on the table by the cauldron. *But that's about to change.*

Blowing a strand of hair off her face, Paige dropped six gardenia blossoms into the mixture in the pot. She added ten dried carnation petals for a jolt of vitality and stirred.

Paige understood why Phoebe resisted taking time off from writing her advice column. Phoebe was becoming something of a celebrity. But even beyond the recognition she was getting for her work, she truly enjoyed it—she loved helping people. Her work at the *Bay Mirror* was similar to her Charmed destiny: She was helping people vanquish demons, though for the column, they were usually inner demons, as opposed to the big, ugly ones that turned up. So it made perfect sense that she wouldn't want to spend time away from people who needed her.

But Piper didn't have a good excuse, which was why it frustrated Paige so much.

Paige added a pinch of faerie fern spore as a catalyst and continued stirring vigorously to activate the potion—and work out her frustration.

The profits from P3, in addition to Phoebe's

salary, were more than enough to pay the household bills, invest, and save. Piper, however, was making decisions as though the sisters were back in the lean days before P3 was operating in the black and Phoebe was gainfully employed. To nullify that argument, Paige had worked the extra jobs to cover some of the vacation expenses. She intended to press the point later, when Wyatt was asleep and Piper could focus.

In the meantime she needed a quick fix for the frayed nerves and weariness a long getaway would cure. She dipped a small glass into the potion and raised it.

"To calm me down and pick me up." Paige drained the glass.

Phoebe stared at the computer monitor, her thoughts as cluttered as the desk in her small office at the *Bay Mirror*, one of San Francisco's daily newspapers. Letters from the lonely, lost, and lovesick were piled around her and sorted by category: definitely answer, maybe answer, and file. She never threw one away.

"Okay, 'Not a Birdbrain,'" Phoebe muttered. She stared at the handwritten letter, trying to formulate a response. "I'd love to recommend buying your insensitive husband a parakeet and telling him to stuff it, but that won't solve your problem."

And Elise Rothman, her editor, would never sign off on the wording. The paper would be inundated with calls from bird lovers outraged over the unintended image of stuffed parakeets.

Phoebe leaned back in her chair to read the letter again. "Not a Birdbrain" was a classic case of a woman who tried too hard to please a man who wouldn't give her credit for anything. Nothing made the guy happy, a situation that screamed for an emancipating solution delivered with a sarcastic sting.

But today Phoebe was at a rare loss for words. Something inspiring or amusing would come to her eventually.

But will it come before my four o'clock deadline? Phoebe wondered, worried.

Lately her creative juices were overtaxed by the grind of writing a daily column and putting together a book proposal. Elise thought Phoebe could sell a manuscript based on the advice published in her column. However, before they could submit the idea, Phoebe had to decide what chapter categories to use and provide examples of her additional commentary.

Yesterday she had taken home hard copies of the book proposal and her half-finished column. She often accomplished more sitting in bed with pen and pad than typing into her laptop. Last night, however, she had wasted time writing a response she finally decided not to use. A woman called "All or Nothing" became angry whenever her boyfriend wanted a minute of hassle-free time to himself. Phoebe thought the woman was way too needy and selfish, but telling her to "grow up, get real, leave the guy alone, or get dumped" was too brutally blunt. She might have to run with it, however, if she couldn't think of a suitable response to "Not a Birdbrain."

Phoebe highlighted the text she had finished and was about to copy it into a separate backup file. A sudden thought made her sit back.

"If 'Not a Birdbrain' goes on strike and stops doing everything, maybe this jerk will realize he's lost without her," Phoebe mused aloud. "A long shot, but it might work."

Phoebe wanted to get the thought written down before she forgot it, but the phone rang.

"Hi, Elise." The lilt in Phoebe's voice didn't match the pained expression on her face. She mentally repeated her unwritten advice to "Not a Birdbrain" as she listened.

Go on strike. Don't do anything. Go on strike . . .

"Is it four o'clock already?" Phoebe tensed. "I'll have it on your desk in ten minutes. Right, not a minute more."

Hanging up, Phoebe hit Enter to begin a new section for her reply to "Not a Birdbrain."

The text she had highlighted to copy vanished.

"What!" Phoebe starred at the blank page on her screen. The column she had just promised to deliver in ten minutes was gone. "Where'd it go?"

Panicking, Phoebe hit Backspace. The page remained blank. Then she remembered that she could Undo a mistake! She found Undo Typing on the menu and clicked on it, but it didn't work. Refusing to accept that her work was irrevocably lost in cyberspace, she clicked again.

Nothing.

Phoebe sagged, realizing that she had panicked and compounded the mistake. However, she didn't have time to beat herself up over it. Elise needed copy Phoebe didn't have.

Although Phoebe knew she could probably retype the column in ten minutes, she'd never remember everything she had written or exactly how she had written it.

"Maybe I don't have to remember . . ." Sitting forward, Phoebe rifled through the file folders on her desk. She had brought the hard copy draft of her column back to the office that morning. She found the file, flipped it open, and groaned when she saw the notes for the book proposal.

She had left the Manor with the wrong file.

Furious with herself, Phoebe tossed the file on the floor and picked up the phone.

"'No, no, no!'" Piper raised the pitch of her voice and furrowed her brow to emphasize the meaning of the words. This was the second read-through of *Good Dog, Bad Dog* since Paige had gone upstairs. Wyatt had pounded the book for more when she finished the first time. "'That's sooooo bad!'"

"Buh!" Wyatt echoed.

"'The floor is all muddy!'" Piper shook her head with mock displeasure. "'What a bad dog!'"

"Buh duh!" Wyatt matched his mother's frown, then grinned.

"Right!" Piper looked from the picture book to the tiny boy on the sofa beside her. "That bad dog got dirty paw prints all over the clean floor."

Wyatt laughed and clapped his hands.

Not exactly the response I wanted, Piper thought.

Every child had to learn to respect the person and property of others to get along in the world. The hammer of social justice came down hard on those who didn't play by the rules. Wyatt had to learn the same lessons as other children, but for different reasons. Her magically superior son wouldn't be harmed if he chose to ignore the laws of modern civilization. The world, however, could suffer greatly at Wyatt's whim if he didn't accept that good was better than bad.

"I know you don't get it yet," Piper said in a motherly coo. "But you will."

Wyatt pounded the book, an impatient signal for Piper to turn the page. The next picture showed the spotted, floppy-eared dog wiping his paws on a mat by the door.

"Now this is better," Piper said with an approving nod. "'That's a *good* dog!'"

Wyatt stared at the picture, content to listen to his mother's animated voice.

"No mud this time," Piper said.

When the phone rang, Piper looked around for the cordless, but she had forgotten to put the handset on the end table. Setting the book aside and gently placing Wyatt on the floor, she ran to answer the phone in the front hall.

"Piper! Thank goodness," Phoebe said, sounding breathless and distraught. "Is Paige there?"

"She's in the attic playing with her good-witch chemistry set." Piper scowled. "Why? What's wrong?"

"Just a little emergency," Phoebe said. "Nothing awful—unless I get fired and can't concentrate on fighting demons or saving Innocents because we're going broke while I'm looking for another job I may not be able to find."

"You were fired?" Piper's eyes widened.

"No," Phoebe said, "but I might be unless Paige orbs to my office with the file folder I left by my bed. A-S-A-P, please! I'll make sure the coast stays clear."

"Okay. I'm on it." Piper hurried toward the stairs as soon as Phoebe hung up. "Paige!"

"What?" Paige hollered down from the attic.

"Phoebe needs the file folder by her bed," Piper yelled back. "Right now."

"Right now this second?" Paige clasped the upper railing and leaned over to look down.

"Immediately," Piper said. She doubted that

Elise would fire the *Bay Mirror*'s celebrity advice columnist. Phoebe was just being dramatic because she needed the file in a hurry. "You have to orb, but Phoebe's guarding the office door."

"I certainly hope so. Nothing ruins a day quicker than a sister who materializes out of thin air in front of witnesses." Paige disappeared to retrieve and deliver the file.

An ominous thump and a squeal reminded Piper that she had left Wyatt alone in the living room—with an open storybook.

"Oops!" Piper raced to the doorway and stopped short to stare. A very large, white cartoon dog with black spots and floppy ears bounded around the room, then sprawled on the floor to plant puppy kisses on Wyatt's face. The carpet and sofa were dotted with big, muddy paw prints.

Wyatt's protective shield wasn't operative, so Piper knew he wasn't in danger. He laughed when the three-dimensional cartoon dog sat back to scratch behind its ear. The live-action toon scene *was* comically surreal.

Piper covered her mouth to muffle a laugh, but she caught the storybook creature's attention anyway. The huge dog lunged toward her with its long, red tongue flapping from the side of its mouth.

"Down, boy!" Piper yelled as the dog sprang.

• • •

"This file?" Paige asked when she finished orbing into Phoebe's office.

"Let's see." Phoebe took the folder from Paige's hand. She flipped it open, scanned the page, and nodded. "This is it. Thanks."

"Happy to help," Paige said. "Gotta go."

"Okay. I can't tell you"—Phoebe looked back at Paige and changed her thought in midsentence—"how did you learn to do that?"

"What?" Paige asked innocently, looking down at her feet. She was floating twelve inches off the floor. "Hover?"

Phoebe nodded.

"An unforeseen side effect of an experimental pick-me-up potion," Paige explained. "I'm still exhausted and stressed, but floating on air."

"I don't want to seem unsympathetic, but"—Phoebe glanced at her watch—"I accidentally erased my computer file for today's column, and I've only got seven minutes left to retype this before I'm in big trouble with Elise."

"You erased your work?" Paige arched an eyebrow and barreled through the opening Phoebe had given her. "So tell me again why you won't take a vacation?"

"Because Elise won't give me two weeks off." Phoebe slid into her desk chair. "That's one of the downsides of having the most popular column in the paper."

"What's another?" Paige asked.

"Writing clever, insightful copy on a deadline

five days a week so 'Ask Phoebe' *stays* the most popular column in the paper." Phoebe opened the file and started typing.

"All work and no play makes Phoebe a dull writer," Paige said as she orbed out.

"Here, Wyatt. Play with these." Piper placed a plastic bowl of lime-flavored Jell-O cubes on Wyatt's high chair tray. He immediately dug in with a chubby hand. "Good boy. Now maybe Mommy can make dinner."

Wyatt wasn't listening. He was fascinated by the green, squishy stuff oozing between his fingers.

Piper set the oven temperature and pulled a package of boneless chicken breasts from the refrigerator. Chicken with wild rice in a white mushroom sauce was a one-dish main course she could throw together in a few minutes, then put in the oven and forget about for an hour. After cleaning splotches of mud off the sofa and carpet, she wasn't in a gourmet mood. She just wanted to sit and relax.

"At least the big white doggie is back where he belongs," Piper muttered softly. Wyatt had put the cartoon pooch back in the book after it pounced on Piper, knocking her down. Muddy paws prints, however, had not put her in peril, giving Wyatt no reason to whisk them back into the book too.

On the plus side, nobody else was aware of

Wyatt's latest trick. Paige had orbed back into the attic from Phoebe's office and hadn't been downstairs since.

"Gurg!" Wyatt laughed.

Piper glanced at her son. Bits of green Jell-O clung to his face and hair. He mashed other green globs on his tray. The messy, harmless play was so normal, she felt a warm glow in her stomach.

Piper placed the chicken breasts over the rice in a glass baking dish. Her only concession to chef's pride was making the sauce from scratch instead of opening a can of cream soup. She poured milk into a saucepan, added butter, and turned to put the milk carton away in the refrigerator. She paused when she realized she had opened the microwave instead.

"Maybe Paige is right," Piper said with a weary sigh.

"About what?" Leo walked into the kitchen and slipped his arms around Piper's waist. He laughed after he looked at his son. "I'd hug Wyatt but he's covered in green glop."

"And you're elected to give him a bath," Piper said.

"In a minute." Leo kissed her neck, then drew back. "What is Paige right about?"

"She's been bugging me about taking a family vacation." As she talked, Piper added the rest of the ingredients to her sauce and stirred slowly.

"Sounds like a great idea." Leo perched on a stool by Wyatt's high chair.

"It is a great idea," Paige said from the doorway. "I don't see that we have a choice."

Phoebe walked in and dropped her briefcase on the floor. "About what?" she asked, coming up behind Paige. "I see you have both feet on the ground."

"Firmly," Paige said. "Apparently the elevating effects were only temporary."

Piper took the pan off the heat and glanced over her shoulder. "Am I missing something?"

"Yes, the point." Paige sat on a stool across from Leo.

"Which is?" Piper spooned the sauce over the chicken and rice, set the saucepan in the sink, and opened the oven door.

"I'm listening." Phoebe reached for an apple in the fruit bowl.

"We *need* a vacation." Paige held up a hand to stay any arguments and kept talking. "I'm not kidding. We're all worn out and stressed out. Mothering a magic baby and giving good advice to total strangers and trying to make up for missing out on a lifetime of witchcraft are not trivial pursuits. If we don't take the time to chill out, we are going to flame out."

As she slid the baking dish into the oven, Piper touched the hot rack, burning herself. She closed the oven and turned to the sink to run cold water on her finger.

"Who's going to save Innocents from demonic evil if we crash and burn?" Paige asked.

"She does have a point," Leo said. He took a damp paper towel from Piper and wiped Wyatt's hands.

"And I've got two weeks off starting now." Phoebe shrugged when all heads turned her way. "Elise thinks my snappy patter has been a little limp lately so she's forcing me to take a brain break."

"What about your column?" Piper asked.

"Spencer Ricks is going to fill in." Phoebe smiled and bit into her apple.

"No worries about him becoming a permanent replacement," Paige observed.

That's true, Piper thought. When a witch doctor had hexed Phoebe to obsess about her career, she thought the cynical, competitive Spencer Ricks wanted her job. She had turned him into a turkey and almost butchered him before the hex was removed and she realized he wasn't a threat. After two weeks of the substitute columnist's caustic advice, the *Bay Mirror*'s readers would be ecstatic to have Phoebe back.

"Looks like Leo and Phoebe agree with me," Paige said. "You're outvoted three to one, Piper. We are taking a family vacation."

Piper no longer had objections. After dealing with the huge, muddy cartoon dog, almost nuking the milk, and burning her hand, she was finally willing to admit she needed a break. Her son, her husband, her sisters, and even the world depended on her ability to stay focused and function perfectly, no matter what the distraction. A vacation was definitely in order.

"Where should we go?" Piper asked, cutting right to the chase. "The Grand Canyon? A movie theme park?"

Leo shook his head. "Wyatt isn't old enough to appreciate a theme park yet."

"I'm open to anything," Phoebe said, "as long as it doesn't require bug spray or sleeping in tents."

"Wyatt would probably also enjoy camping more when he's older," Piper agreed.

"I'd like to make a pilgrimage to Salem, Massachusetts," Paige announced. "To explore our witch heritage."

"Been there, done that," Phoebe said. "We already learned the basic tenets of natural magic in colonial Virginia."

"Absolutely not." Piper wiped the high chair tray with a sponge. "If I'm going on vacation, I don't want to spend it in musty museums and tourist traps devoted to the persecution of witches."

"But I do," Paige protested. "I've never been to Salem. Besides, we wouldn't be spending *every* minute taking tours. There's got to be other things to do for fun in Massachusetts. Especially this time of year—summer is beautiful there."

"Antiquing!" Phoebe said, grinning. "Maybe Piper can find pieces that match our crystal and china."

"To replace the broken ones I'm always complaining about?" Piper asked. Some of the family heirlooms dated back to New England colonial times. The idea was appealing—to her. "I'm sure Wyatt will love that," she added sarcastically.

"Probably not." Leo lifted Wyatt out of the high chair and held him at arm's length to avoid getting sticky Jell-O bits on his shirt. "But we can see every exhibit in modern day Salem in a couple of days. Then we could spend the rest of our vacation at the beach."

"Wyatt would love that," Piper said.

"Works for me," Phoebe agreed.

"Great!" Paige jumped off her stool. "I'll make all the arrangements. You guys don't have to worry about a thing. Just start packing."

Chapter

2

"I am *really* sorry," Paige said as she climbed into the rear seat of the rented minivan. They were finally driving south to Salem, Massachusetts, from Manchester, New Hampshire, after wasting several hours in the San Francisco airport.

"That's four times you've apologized, Paige." Phoebe glanced back from the front passenger seat. "It's not your fault the plane was late taking off."

"I know," Paige said. "But I'm the one who had the brilliant idea of flying into Manchester instead of Boston because the tickets were cheaper. The Boston flight took off on time."

Leo buckled himself into the driver's seat. "Nobody's going to give you a hard time for saving money."

"Especially me," Piper said, strapping Wyatt into his car seat by the window in the middle row. "I'm going to spend every dollar we saved in an antique store."

"This one had some good stuff." Phoebe flicked her hand toward the rustic red barn they had just left.

Paige looked at the sign painted on the side of the barn: COUNTRY COOKIN' AN' 'TIQUES. The old-style lettering was identical to the faded bill-board Phoebe had spotted from the interstate. Floodlights illuminated the words as twilight surrendered to darkness.

The roadside business combined good junk with good food for hungry, treasure-hunting travelers. Established in 1934, the sprawling antique shop and restaurant was located ten miles from the I-93 exit. The scenic secondary highway that followed a narrow river and cut through a dense forest had been a main route before the interstate was built.

Phoebe held up a set of salt and pepper shakers shaped like frogs and painted brown. "These were a steal for three dollars."

"More like highway robbery," Leo said. He ducked when Phoebe cuffed his shoulder and waited until she sat back before starting the engine.

"They appeal to my inner witch," Phoebe countered.

"I think they're adorable," Piper said. She pulled the side door closed and buckled herself in. "It's just too bad 'Tiques didn't have any pieces in our china and crystal patterns. The food was good, though."

"I've never had littleneck steamer clams before," Phoebe said. "A couple were a little gritty, but they tasted okay."

"Dipping them in butter rinsed the grit off, didn't it?" Piper asked.

"Most of it." Phoebe nodded. "Is that why raccoons wash their food?"

"Do raccoons eat clams?" Leo asked.

Paige closed her eyes and nodded off to the comforting sounds of small talk that had nothing to do with mortal danger or demonic villains.

Maybe fate took a hint from Elise, Paige thought, *and decided to give us a Charmed break.*

Phoebe settled back for the drive south to Salem and stared out the side window. With only the sliver of a waning moon in the night sky, it was too dark to see anything beyond the range of the headlights.

Everyone was tired after a long day and a big dinner. They had only been back on the road a few minutes, but Paige and Wyatt had already fallen asleep. Piper and Leo had lapsed into the relieved silence of parents who didn't get enough peace and quiet.

"Look at that," Leo said, his voice a gentle ripple that barely disturbed the tranquility inside the van. "A covered bridge."

"On this road?" Phoebe glanced out the windshield.

Spotlights on the ground lit up the old-fashioned wooden structure that spanned the two-lane highway ahead. A historical marker noted that the bridge had been built in 1843, restored in 1930, and reinforced in 1957. Since the highway narrowed to fit through the old bridge, the speed limit was reduced to twenty miles per hour. Two vehicles barely had room to pass without scraping paint.

"We didn't cross this bridge when we got off the interstate, did we?" Phoebe asked, craning to look back as the van cleared the structure.

"Nope." Acting as the designated navigator, Piper opened the road atlas and turned on a flashlight.

"I must have turned the wrong way out of the parking lot," Leo said, sighing.

"Yep." Piper ran her finger over the atlas page. "We're headed southwest—away from I-93."

"So we have to turn around and go back?" Leo sounded annoyed.

"Not necessarily," Piper said, still studying the map. "If we keep going, we'll intercept another secondary road that will take us back to the interstate."

"Good," Leo said, "because I hate backtracking. It's a waste of time and miles."

"We're going to waste time and miles no matter what we do." Piper looked up with an impish grin. "This route adds forty miles to the trip."

Leo shrugged. "Well, I'd rather waste time and miles going forward, not back."

"I don't mind the extra driving," Paige piped up sleepily from the backseat, "but it's too dark to see this gorgeous scenery."

"We could stop overnight somewhere," Phoebe suggested. "It doesn't matter if we get to Salem tonight or tomorrow. We're not on anyone's schedule but our own."

"Right," Paige said. "And since our flight was delayed we don't have hotel rooms in Salem anymore."

"We don't?" Phoebe looked back. "I thought you made reservations."

"I did, but I didn't secure them with a credit card," Paige explained. "So the hotel gave our rooms to someone else when we didn't show up by six o'clock. My bad—again."

"Not so bad," Phoebe said. "At least we didn't already pay for them."

"What about tomorrow night?" Leo asked.

"Let's worry about that tomorrow," Piper said.

"Wow, this vacation has already mellowed you out! How far to the next town, Piper?" Paige asked.

"Looks like ten miles or so to Cairn," Piper answered. "But the town is so small it's just a tiny black dot on the map. What if it doesn't have a motel?"

"Hang on." Phoebe dug into her bag and pulled out an electronic traveler's aid she had purchased for the trip. She punched in the name of the town, the highway, and the direction they were driving. Then she hit the Hotel/Motel button to find the nearest accommodations.

"The Yankee Bear," Phoebe said, reading the information off the small screen. "Bed-and-breakfast, two miles north of Cairn."

Piper turned off the flashlight. "Maybe we should wait and see what this place looks like before we get too excited."

Several minutes later Phoebe spotted the wooden sign for the bed-and-breakfast on an expansive lawn. According to the sign, the Yankee Bear in Cairn, New Hampshire, had been in business for almost one hundred and fifty years. Ida Thornwood was now, but apparently had not always been, the sole owner and proprietor. Her name was off center, indicating that there had been an additional name that was now painted over. A Vacancy shingle hung from the sign's lower edge.

"It looks perfect," Paige said as Leo steered the van up a long, tree-lined driveway.

"Good enough for tonight, anyway," Piper said.

Most of the large, three-story house was invisible in the dark night, but lights on either side of the door and a double-globe lamp by the steps cast a welcoming glow over the front porch. Pots of red geraniums hung from the overhanging roof braces. Colorful, trailing petunias cascaded from a flower box under a narrow, small-paned window by the door. A porch swing, Adirondack chairs, and a low table invited the road-weary to stop and rest.

Rather than wake Wyatt in case they had to move on, Phoebe volunteered to act as scout and ask about rooms.

"I'll go with you," Paige said. "I have a cramp in my foot I need to work out."

The red front door swung inward and stood open. Phoebe paused before the screen door to peer inside. A lush Boston fern sat on an antique table in the entry hall. An ornate mirror hung on the wall above it and an antique straight chair stood beside it. The registration counter at the end of the foyer was made of dark, polished wood. Several brochures advertising nearby tourist sites were tucked into a wooden rack on the wall by the antique counter.

"Where is everyone?" Paige asked.

"Maybe we have to ring the bell," Phoebe said, pointing toward the counter as she stepped inside.

"I insist, Nathaniel," an unseen woman said. Her voice had the gruff timbre of age. "I'm going to close the Yankee Bear for three days just as I do every month. There's no point you being here with nothing to do."

"But you can't close *this* weekend, Ida," a

man argued in a soft baritone. "What about the solar eclipse on Sunday?"

"The moon will still blot out the sun whether the inn is open or not." The woman—who Phoebe assumed was Ida Thornwood—sounded exasperated.

"And you'll lose a lot of business you can't afford to lose," Nathaniel pressed.

"That's my business, not yours," the elderly woman said as she bustled into the foyer from a front sitting room on the left. She stopped when she saw Phoebe and Paige.

The impression of hospitality conveyed by the porch setting was muted by Ida Thornwood's brusque demeanor. Wearing a long skirt and boots with a long-sleeved flannel shirt over a T-shirt, the small, wizened owner of the Yankee Bear looked to be about seventy. Her dark eyes flicked from Phoebe to Paige.

"Sorry, we're closed." Ida's curt tone was dismissive. She glanced away and stepped behind the counter, as though the sisters had already left.

Phoebe's immediate impulse was to go someplace where paying customers were not an inconvenience. Paige, however, wasn't ready to back down.

"The door was open," Paige said.

"My mistake," the elderly woman retorted. "I'll lock it as soon as you're gone."

Phoebe noticed the young man watching from the arched sitting-room doorway. Blue jeans and a denim work shirt brought out the blue in his eyes, even from across the room. Tall and muscular, with brown hair and rugged good looks, he stood with a backpack slung over his shoulder. Catching Phoebe's eye, he shrugged in apology for his employer's rude manner.

Nathaniel, I presume, Phoebe thought.

Paige's attention was riveted on Mrs. Thornwood. "We just want to stay for one night."

"It's too late to turn them away, Ida," Nathaniel said, stepping out of the shadows. "It's only one room."

Phoebe noted the subtle spark of interest in Paige's eyes when she finally noticed Nathaniel. However, not even a good-natured, gorgeous guy could divert a Halliwell locked in a contest of wills.

"Two rooms, actually," Paige said, addressing Ida. "We have two more adults and a baby in the car."

"A baby?" Ida gave in with a resigned sigh and put a registration form and a ballpoint pen on the countertop. "Fill this out, and I'll need your credit card—for one night."

"Thanks." Paige smiled with satisfaction.

"I'll go tell Piper and Leo," Phoebe said. As she turned to leave, a younger woman raced in from a small hallway at the back of the house.

"Grandma, I can't find—" The woman halted, her hand flying to her throat when she saw the strangers.

"Not now, Harriet," Ida snapped, waving her granddaughter away. "Go back to your room. I'll be there as soon as I'm finished."

Harriet just stood, gawking at the newcomers. She was also wearing a long skirt and T-shirt, but her feet were bare. She pulled the edges of a bulky sweater closed, as though to protect herself. Her dark hair was pulled back and fastened at the nape of her neck in a tight bun. Although she had a clear complexion and large doe eyes accented with dark lashes, the young woman's middle-age wardrobe and severe hairstyle masked a pretty face and trim figure.

Is Harriet trying to be unattractive? Phoebe wondered. *Or is that her grandmother's idea?*

"Now, Harriet," Ida said.

As the young woman ran back down the hall, Phoebe's eyes flashed with indignation. The relationship between the old woman and her granddaughter was none of Phoebe's business as a mortal busybody, but she had been helping people as a Charmed One too long. An Innocent was an Innocent.

"Is she okay?" Phoebe asked Ida, trying to sound concerned rather than angry or accusatory.

"She's fine," Ida said. "Just shy."

"I've worked here three months," the young man explained, "and Harriet rarely talks to me."

Phoebe had the feeling Nathaniel was trying to reassure her. *Probably so Ida won't lose paying customers*, she thought.

"You won't be working here at all if you don't stop talkin' now and help these people with their bags," Ida huffed.

"Yes, ma'am." Nathaniel dropped his backpack on a chair and headed toward the door.

Phoebe found Nathaniel's polite deference to the cranky old woman endearing, but she couldn't shake the idea that something more than acute shyness was troubling Harriet.

Then again, it had been a long day, and she was tired. Maybe she had just overreacted to a normal exchange between an old woman and her timid granddaughter.

Paige had only napped for a few minutes in the van, but that was enough to keep her wide awake now. She punched her pillow and turned on her side, but when she closed her eyes, her brain clicked into high gear.

Would the Salem museums accurately reflect the town's ill-treatment of witches four hundred years ago? Had anyone remembered to turn off the coffee pot before they left for the airport? Was Harriet's fear of strangers indicative of something worse, as Phoebe thought? Phoebe had gone to bed fretting about it but had fallen sound asleep despite her concerns. A natural empathy for people with problems had served Phoebe well as a psychology student, an advice columnist, and a Charmed One. Even in the absence of magical or mortal wrongdoing, she couldn't help worrying about the lost and helpless.

"So why am I the one who's losing sleep?" Paige muttered. She gave up and sat up.

Reading might shift her mind down to a drowsy idle, but she had left her paperback in the van. Leo had locked the car and kept the keys, so she couldn't get it.

There might be books or magazines in the downstairs sitting room for guests, Paige thought as she slipped out of bed and threw on a bathrobe. If there wasn't anything to read, she could at least browse the brochures in the rack by the registration counter. She put on socks, but left her shoes by the bed. Since the door hinges were well-oiled and silent, Phoebe didn't stir as Paige left the room.

Low-wattage bulbs in antique fixtures lit the second-floor hallway. The floorboards creaked with old-house complaint as Paige padded down the stairs to the landing and on down to the front foyer. Suddenly worried about waking someone, she decided not to search for a book. As she stepped toward the brochure rack on the wall, a key turned in the front-door lock. The door opened, and the foyer lights flicked on.

Paige exchanged surprised stares with the good-looking handyman she had met earlier. He had introduced himself to Leo as Nathaniel Coffey.

"I thought you left for the night," Paige said.

"I forgot my books." Nathaniel pointed at the backpack on the chair where he had left it. "I got all the way back into town before I remembered."

"I'm surprised you don't live here," Paige said, making casual conversation. Had the backpack slipped his mind because he was thinking about something—or someone—else? "How often does Mrs. Thornwood rent out all twelve rooms?"

Earlier Mrs. Thornwood had unlocked the case on the wall behind the registration counter to remove keys for the rooms they had rented. Ten additional keys hung on the remaining numbered hooks. Paige assumed that no one else was staying at the Yankee Bear tonight.

"Often enough. But a word of advice," Nathaniel said as he picked up his backpack. "Ida hates being called Mrs. Thornwood."

"Warning noted," Paige said. It would seem odd for an elderly woman to object to being addressed with respect, but Ida Thornwood was blatantly contrary.

"And she doesn't want anyone else living here full-time." Nathaniel moved to the registration counter and set down his backpack. He didn't seem in a hurry to leave.

"I got the impression she doesn't want anyone staying here anytime," Paige said.

"Only three days out of every twenty-eight." Nathaniel smiled. "Like clockwork."

Another Ida oddity, Paige thought, intrigued.

"Ida isn't very friendly, but she's usually civil. She's just"—Nathaniel hesitated, groping for an acceptable way to describe Ida's dour disposition—"eccentric."

"And Harriet's shy," Paige added, info-fishing for Phoebe. Nathaniel had worked at the Yankee Bear for three months. He would have noticed if anything was amiss between Harriet and her grandmother.

"Very shy." Picking up the backpack again, Nathaniel turned to leave.

But he's not talking, Paige thought.

"One sec before you turn off the lights." Paige scanned the rack of brochures and pulled out a pamphlet for a place called Mystic Knoll. "Okay," she said, smiling. "You can go now."

"Are you interested in the occult?" Nathaniel asked.

"Just curious," Paige answered warily, taken aback by his reference to the paranormal. "Are you?"

"Yes, but not as a believer. I'm a grad student at the University of New Hampshire," Nathaniel explained.

"They have a Department of the Occult?" Paige asked. His scholarly credentials were not as surprising—or alarming—as his course of study. She *was* a witch, after all.

"I'm working on a Ph.D. in American Culture, specifically folklore," he said.

"A Ph.D." Paige was impressed. "So you're not really a handyman."

"No, I'm a handyman," Nathaniel said. "I have to do something to pay my expenses while I'm researching my thesis."

"A thesis on what?" Paige asked.

"The psychological effects of local legends on the people within a community."

Paige raised an eyebrow. She had never thought about how people who came in constant contact with the inexplicable might be influenced by it.

Which explains why Nathaniel is working on a graduate degree and I'm not, she thought.

"How are they affected?" Paige asked with genuine interest.

Nathaniel leaned against the counter. "Believe it or not, most people completely reject scientific explanations that shatter their myths."

"They do?" Paige blinked. She would have thought the opposite was true.

Nathaniel nodded. "I know, it's mind-boggling, but a lot of people *want* to believe in magic. Half the folks in Cairn think Mystic Knoll has some kind of weird power." He hesitated, holding her gaze. "But you're not like that."

"Delusional?" Paige rephrased so she could answer honestly and pulled two more brochures from the rack, one for Homer's Bait & Boats and another for the Cairn Historical Society. "No, I am not delusional."

"You should take the Mystic Knoll tour anyway." Nathaniel tapped the pamphlet. "They've
carbon-dated pottery shards from the site at four
thousand years old. The stone configurations are
more random, but they may have had an astronomical function similar to Stonehenge in Great
Britain."

"Really? I might do that." Paige yawned.
"Sorry. It's the hour, not the company."

"I hope so." Nathaniel picked up his backpack. "Maybe we could have dinner tomorrow."
When Paige hesitated, he hastened to add, "To
discuss what you think about Mystic Knoll."

"I'd love to, but we're leaving in the morning," Paige said with an apologetic shrug.

She didn't want to turn down the offer. Aside
from being the most attractive man she'd met in
weeks, Nathaniel was intelligent, caring, and
easy to talk to. His academic interest in the paranormal was intriguing, but she couldn't ask her
family to put their vacation on hold so she could
keep a dinner date.

"Oh, right. One night. I forgot." Nathaniel
strode to the door and looked back before he
closed it behind him. "That's my rotten luck."

"Mine too." Paige sighed as his key turned in
the lock. She watched through the narrow front
window until his headlights disappeared down
the drive. Then, as she turned to go upstairs, a
pattering sound drew her attention back to the
porch.

The staccato rhythm intensified as Paige rushed to the window. The porch lights were still on. She pressed her face against the middle pane and looked down as dozens of large, winged bugs smashed into the house. The fatal cadence increased as dozens became hundreds. The main swarm hit with such force Paige's heart lurched. She jumped back as bugs splattered against the window, darkening the small panes.

A moment passed before Paige realized the thumping noise coming from the back of the house wasn't being generated by the suicidal swarm. She crept back to the counter and down the hallway Harriet had used earlier. It ended at the doorway to a large country kitchen. Another hallway connected from the left a few feet before the door.

The frenzied beat of kamikaze bugs tapered off and the thumping sound stopped suddenly.

Paige paused where the two halls joined, shivering in the eerie stillness. She was about to retrace her steps when a door in the adjacent hallway opened. Light poured into the hall as Ida stepped out.

"Are you coming back, Grandma?" Harriet asked from inside the room. She sounded frantic but unharmed, and anxious for Ida to return.

"After I check the windows. Go to sleep." Ida flicked a switch, turning on an overhead light as she closed the bedroom door. She took a step toward Paige before she noticed her. "You looking for something?"

"Something to read." Paige held up the pamphlets.

"The stairs are that way." Ida motioned toward the foyer.

Paige had faced down too many demons to be intimidated by a scrawny old lady with an acerbic attitude. She stood her ground. "Are swarms of bugs with a death wish common around here?"

"Mystic Knoll is right down the road," Ida explained. "Dang place makes the wildlife go crazy sometimes."

Paige nodded as though that theory made sense. She wouldn't have pegged Ida as someone who gave credence to the paranormal. Maybe Ida knew the Mystic Knoll explanation was bunk, but she just wanted to avoid a lengthy discussion.

"Did the noise scare Harriet?" Paige pressed.

"She has nightmares," Ida said, "and I'd like to check for broken windows before the sun comes up."

"I'll see you in the morning, then." Nodding her good night, Paige headed back to her room. She wished Phoebe's laptop wasn't locked in the van with her book so she could access the Internet.

Something had driven those bugs to self-destruct en masse.

Chapter
3

Piper steadied her coffee cup as she sat on the porch swing. Leo sat at the other end, with Wyatt safely tucked under his arm. As soon as she was settled, Leo pushed the swing into motion.

"Eeee!" Wyatt laughed.

Piper smiled. To the casual observer, her son was a normal, happy child with proud but average parents. As a rule, that was an illusion she didn't dare indulge. Their reality was too hazardous.

"Wyatt likes that," Paige said, moving her head in time to the rocking swing. She sat in one of the low-slung Adirondack chairs, reading a brochure.

"A thrill a minute." Leo grinned. "We're working our way up to teeter-totters."

Piper sipped her coffee and sighed with content. "I could get used to this."

"What 'this' exactly?" Phoebe asked. She

lounged in the other Adirondack chair with her feet propped on the low table.

Lest there be big ears lurking about, Piper didn't voice what was really on her mind. They had just spent twenty-four hours without being threatened by some despicable evil that was intent on kidnapping Wyatt or destroying them, an Innocent, or the world. So maybe it *was* possible to get away from everything after all! Until events proved otherwise, she intended to enjoy every unexciting, ordinary minute of her vacation.

"Having someone else make the bed and breakfast," Piper said. "Morning coffee on a porch swing followed by a whole day with nothing pressing to do. Except go shopping."

Paige looked up. "I thought we were going to Salem."

"Let's go to Salem tomorrow." Piper held up Phoebe's electronic travel aid. "According to this gadget, Cairn has a bunch of antique shops."

"Seriously?" Paige asked. "You really want to stay?"

"Yeah." Piper nodded. "This town is so far off the beaten path, I might actually find some of the china pieces we're missing."

"And the sooner we get going, the sooner we can take Wyatt to the park," Leo said, standing up.

The instant the swing stopped, Wyatt started to cry.

"Don't worry, buddy." Leo scooped the boy up and held him high in both hands. "We'll have fun rummaging through all that old junk. Maybe *we'll* find a Buck Rogers lunch box or a Roy Rogers cowboy hat."

"Careful, Leo," Phoebe admonished. "You're dating yourself. Besides, you don't look old enough to know who Buck Rogers and Roy Rogers were."

"Who were they?" Paige asked.

"A 1930s space hero and a 1940s singing cowboy," Leo answered.

"A Buck Rogers lunch box would probably break the bank," Piper said, standing up. She took Wyatt while Leo went to get the diaper bag from their room. "Are you sure you two won't mind hanging around New Hampshire another day?"

"Actually, no," Phoebe said. "I don't mind."

"It's all right with me, too." Paige took a doughnut off the tray on the table. "I'll find something to do. Take the Mystic Knoll tour, have dinner with Nathaniel—"

"With the handyman?" Piper wasn't being judgmental. She was, as always, amazed at Paige's ability to attract handsome men no matter where she was or what she was doing.

"Graduate student working on his Ph.D. at the University of New Hampshire," Paige explained.

Phoebe's eyes widened. "Did he ask you out in your sleep?"

"Midnight encounter in the front hall," Paige said.

"Whatever. Have fun. I'm out of here." Resting Wyatt on her hip, Piper hurried toward the van. "Bye!"

Piper's step was as light as her heart. She had forgotten how it felt to have the weight of the world lifted from her shoulders.

She felt free.

Phoebe sighed as Piper and Leo drove off for a day of family fun with Wyatt. She couldn't remember when she had seen Piper so rested and relaxed. The Yankee Bear had had the opposite affect on her. Phoebe sensed something sinister that went far beyond concern for a timid young woman, but she couldn't define it or explain why the feeling was strong.

"Want to check out Mystic Knoll with me?" Paige reached for the last apple-cinnamon doughnut, then changed her mind.

"We don't have a car," Phoebe said, taking advantage of the convenient excuse. She wasn't as eager to explore rural New Hampshire as her sisters. Between crushing deadlines and a heavy schedule of personal appearances, her life as a popular newspaper columnist was so hectic that now she just wanted to sit and read.

"It's just down the road," Paige said. "We can walk."

"Thanks, but I'll pass." Phoebe glanced at the lone doughnut on the tray. She had been fighting a carbohydrate craving for the past half hour.

Her willpower finally collapsed on typical tourist grounds: She was on vacation.

As Phoebe reached for the doughnut, Harriet burst through the front door and swept the tray up off the table.

"Wait a minute—" Phoebe spoke on reflex.

Harriet froze with a white-knuckled grip on the tray. "I have to pick up the dishes."

"Okay," Phoebe said, smiling. She had reacted without taking into consideration Harriet's fragile personality. To counter the young woman's unease, she clasped her hands with a pleading look. "But could I *please* have that last doughnut?"

Paige watched without saying anything, as though she knew a sudden sound might send Harriet scurrying for cover.

Harriet nodded and held out the tray, revealing a large bruise under her short shirtsleeve.

Pretending not to notice the injury, Phoebe took the doughnut. "Thanks, Harriet."

"Sure." With another quick nod, Harriet put Leo's and Piper's empty coffee cups on the tray and rushed back inside.

"She has a huge bruise on her arm," Phoebe told Paige. "Any theories about how she got it?"

"Throwing herself against a wall, maybe," Paige said.

"What?" That wasn't the answer Phoebe was expecting. Her first inclination was to blame Ida. "What makes you say that?"

"I heard something banging against a wall when I went downstairs last night," Paige explained. "I think Harriet freaked out when the bugs started battering the house."

"Bugs?" Phoebe frowned. "What bugs?"

Paige straightened up, scanned the porch floor, and glanced at the window. "She must have cleaned up last night."

"Who?" Phoebe asked, getting more confused.

"Ida." Paige leaned to look through the porch railing and pointed at the lawn below. "Those bugs."

Phoebe stood up to look. Piles of smashed insect bodies littered the grass. "That's a lot of dead bugs."

"Millions with nothing to live for, apparently." Paige sat back. "Ida said Mystic Knoll makes the wildlife around here go crazy sometimes."

"When did she say that?" Phoebe asked. The old woman's conversation had been limited to a grudging "good morning" when she had brought out the doughnuts and coffee.

"I ran into her coming out of Harriet's room last night," Paige explained. "She said Harriet has nightmares."

"Do you believe her?" Phoebe took a bite of the doughnut and washed it down with cold coffee.

"Don't know. You're the psychologist, so that's your department." Paige drained her cup and set it on the table. She brushed doughnut crumbs off her jeans as she stood up. "If there's anything strange about Mystic Knoll, maybe I'll get a clue when I take the tour."

"Maybe," Phoebe said absently, finishing the doughnut. "I'll see what I can find out about Harriet."

Neither one of them questioned the impulse to investigate. Phoebe couldn't turn away from a person in need, and Paige couldn't resist a mystery. There might be logical, harmless explanations for the suicidal bugs and Harriet's emotional state, but they had to find out.

Nathaniel rounded the corner of the house. He wore a Red Sox baseball cap and carried a rake and an old bushel basket made of wooden slats and wire. "Morning, ladies."

"Hey, Nathaniel!" Paige waved. "What are you doing here? I thought Ida gave you three days off."

"I only take off when she closes the Yankee Bear," Nathaniel said, looking directly at Paige. "But since you're still here, I don't mind being here too."

I don't think I can stand the sugar rush, Phoebe thought, hiding an amused smile. At least her inner truth meter wasn't clanging with alarm. Nathaniel meant what he said. "Excuse me, but I could use another cup of coffee."

"Take your time," Paige said with a pointed look.

Phoebe assumed her sister wanted a few minutes alone with Nathaniel to confirm their dinner date. Taking the hint and their empty coffee cups, she walked back to the kitchen. Ida wasn't there. Harriet was transferring clean dishes from the dishwasher to the cupboards.

"Is there more coffee, Harriet?" Phoebe asked.

With her back to the door, Harriet hadn't heard Phoebe come in. At the question, she jumped with a muffled cry.

"Sorry," Phoebe said. "I didn't mean to startle you."

Harriet nervously wiped her hands on her apron, then pointed to a coffee urn on the counter. "Coffee's there."

"Thanks." Phoebe poured herself another cup and paused to take a sip. She cast an appreciative glance around the spacious kitchen.

Sunlight streamed through the windows in the back door and over the sink. A brick fireplace with a raised hearth filled half of the outside wall. The center of the room was dominated by a large butcher-block island, and a built-in table with booths filled one corner. Seat cushions in a country patchwork pattern matched the curtains.

Noting the jar of pens and pencils, notebooks, telephone directory, and phone on the table, Phoebe guessed that the kitchen doubled as an office.

"Piper would be in her glory here," Phoebe said. "She's a chef."

"Uh-huh." Harriet didn't look toward Phoebe as she unloaded more dishes.

"Your sign says the Yankee Bear is one hundred fifty years old." Phoebe hoped her casual interest would dispel some of Harriet's anxiety. "Has it always been in your family?"

"Grandpa bought it," Harriet mumbled, then cleared her throat. "In 1950," she said in a stronger voice.

"I see." Phoebe nodded, taking another sip of coffee. She was afraid Harriet would clam up again if she pressed too hard.

"He's dead," Harriet added.

"Oh, that's too bad," Phoebe said. The disclosure explained the name that had been painted over on the sign, but it also raised another question: Why had Ida erased the reference to her dead husband?

"No guests allowed in the kitchen," Ida said as she came into the room.

Phoebe noted that the woman walked with a brisk bustle. The message in Ida's posture was unmistakable: She was in charge and wanted everyone to know.

And her timing is terrible, Phoebe thought. Harriet had seemed to be opening up a little before her grandmother interrupted.

Harriet grabbed a stack of dishes and hurried back to the cupboard without uttering another word.

Guess that conversation is over, Phoebe thought

with irritation and dismay. Her suspicions that Ida mistreated her granddaughter seemed more and more likely.

"When do you folks plan on leaving?" Ida asked.

"Later," Phoebe said. She didn't want to confront Ida about extending their stay without backup. Paige had told Ida they wanted rooms for only one night, and staying longer was Piper's idea. "Piper and Leo went into town, and Paige wants to take the Mystic Knoll tour."

"You'll be here until this afternoon?" Ida's scowl deepened with displeasure.

"Yes, and I need a shower," Phoebe said. *We will be here until this afternoon,* she told herself as she left the kitchen, *and until tomorrow morning, too.*

The second and third floors each had six rooms and two shared bathrooms. The door to the bath across from the room she shared with Paige was locked. She put her ear to the door. The shower water was running.

"Hello?" Phoebe called and knocked. She hadn't heard Paige come in, but they were the only guests at the inn. "Are you in there, Paige?"

"I'll be done in a few minutes!" Paige called back.

"No rush!" Phoebe walked down the hall to the other bathroom on the floor. By the time she finished dressing in white shorts and a spaghetti-strap top, Paige had left the inn.

Grabbing a towel and the thriller novel she had started reading on the plane, Phoebe went back outside. She settled in one of three wooden lawn chairs by a flower garden in full, exuberant bloom. She had barely started reading when she heard Nathaniel shout.

"Harriet?" The handyman strode across the lawn. He paused and cupped his hands around his mouth. "Harriet!"

Phoebe marked her place with the Mystic Knoll brochure she had borrowed from Paige and let the book fall in her lap. She sat up when Nathaniel hurried toward her.

"Have you seen Harriet?" Nathaniel asked.

"Not since I left her in the kitchen about thirty minutes ago," Phoebe said. "Is she missing?"

"Nothing to worry about," Nathaniel said. "We'll find her."

The sound of a motor drew Phoebe's gaze toward the driveway. Ida sat behind the wheel of an old pickup truck. She slowed the truck and shouted out the passenger side window.

"I'll check the road!" Ida didn't wait for Nathaniel to respond. She gunned the engine and drove toward the highway.

"Is Harriet on foot?" Phoebe asked.

Nathaniel nodded and turned toward the woods.

Phoebe dropped her book on the lawn chair and jogged after him. "She couldn't have gone far."

Nathaniel paused, frowning uncertainly. "What are you doing?"

"Going with you to help find Harriet," Phoebe said. Nathaniel was obviously worried about the young woman. He was also, apparently, suspicious of her motives. "Four eyes are better than two."

"You don't know these woods or Harriet's habits," Nathaniel said. "And I need to be looking for her, not talking to you."

"Then you'd better get moving," Phoebe said. "And I'll be right behind you."

Realizing she would not be dissuaded, Nathaniel led the way through a break in the fence. "If you get lost, you're on your own."

Phoebe followed Nathaniel down a worn path through the trees. She kept quiet as he called Harriet's name. A stranger's voice might frighten the runaway. When the trail forked, Nathaniel turned right without hesitation.

"How do you know this is the right way?" Phoebe asked, pushing aside a leafy branch.

"I don't," Nathaniel explained. "She went this way the last time."

"Does she disappear often?" Phoebe asked. When Nathaniel didn't answer, she tried to allay his reservations. "I don't mean to meddle, Nathaniel. I handle people's troubles professionally, and I'm worried about Harriet. Ida is such a strong personality—"

"And very protective," Nathaniel interjected.

The supportive answer told Phoebe that Nathaniel didn't perceive Ida as a threat. She phrased her next question with that in mind, being careful not to sound accusatory. "Because Harriet's so shy?"

"Are you a psychiatrist?" Nathaniel asked.

"I have a degree in psychology," Phoebe assured him, telling the truth without being specific.

Nathaniel stopped and looked back. He searched her gaze, trying to decide whether or not to trust her.

"And I make my living helping people solve their problems," Phoebe added. "I'd like to help Harriet."

"I'm not sure that's possible," Nathaniel said. "Harriet isn't just shy. She has . . . periods of erratic behavior."

"I don't understand," Phoebe prompted.

"Screaming, tearing her clothes, throwing things," Nathaniel explained. "I once found her bashing the utility shed with a shovel. She attacked me when I tried to stop her."

"How awful," Phoebe said.

"Harriet can't help it, but it's one good reason why we have to find her before someone else does," Nathaniel said.

"What's the other?" Phoebe asked.

"She might hurt herself." Nathaniel called Harriet's name and scanned the woods as he plunged ahead.

Nathaniel's information supported Paige's theory that Harriet got the bruise when she threw herself against a wall. It also raised more questions. Since Phoebe might not have another opportunity, she wanted to ask them all now.

Phoebe asked the obvious question first. "Is it a medical condition?"

Nathaniel stopped to peer at a large fallen log, then sighed. He stared at the ground for a moment, as though trying to decide whether or not to confide in her.

"I can't help if I don't know what the problem is," Phoebe prodded.

"Funny," Nathaniel said. "That's what I told Ida when I asked questions about Harriet two months ago. I'd only been working here a month, but Ida must have sensed I really cared."

"So do I," Phoebe said.

Nathaniel nodded. "Harriet's had fits since she was born, but they've never found anything physical to explain them."

A hideous screech sounded ahead.

"She's at old man Dalton's place." Nathaniel broke into a run.

Phoebe had trouble keeping up. She stayed on the path until she saw Nathaniel cut through the trees toward a clearing. Briars scratched her legs when she veered off the trail after him.

"Get off my property, freak!" a man yelled. "Get out of here!"

Phoebe saw Harriet crouched by a stone wall.

The young woman's face was streaked with dirt. Vines and leaves were tangled in her hair. Harriet shook her fists and shrieked at a scruffy-looking old man wearing coveralls and a cowboy hat.

"Get!" The old man threw a rock. It missed Harriet and sailed over the stone wall. "Get out of here before I call the sheriff!"

"Calm down, Jed!" Nathaniel raised his voice, but stayed calm, as he entered a cluttered yard. He skirted a rusted old car and piles of discarded junk as he walked toward Harriet. "I'll get her."

"Ida should keep that loony locked up," Jed Dalton huffed.

"Be careful, Jed," Nathaniel said. "Some folks say the same thing about you."

When Harriet saw Nathaniel, she bolted. The young man was quicker. He threw his arms around the woman, pinning hers to her sides. She fought, shrieking and kicking for several seconds before her crazed expression blanked and she passed out.

Phoebe waited at the tree line as Nathaniel lifted Harriet's limp form. He had taken effective control, and her presence might just complicate matters.

"Let's go," Nathaniel said as he passed Phoebe.

Phoebe fell into step behind the student handyman again. He carried Harriet back to the fallen log before he stopped to rest. Phoebe perched atop the rough bark as he gently placed the unconscious woman on the ground. He sat down, cradling Harriet's head in his lap.

"After that," Phoebe said, referring to the old man's cruel taunts, "it's easy to understand why Harriet avoids people."

"To be blunt, she's thought of as the town weirdo," Nathaniel said. "Everyone has either seen one of her episodes or heard about them. That's why Ida finally decided to home school her when she was fourteen, to protect her from harm and humiliation. That was six years ago."

"Harriet hasn't gone anywhere in six years?" Phoebe was aghast.

"Not without her grandmother and not very often," Nathaniel said. "Ida only tolerates having me around because she and Harriet can't handle the heavy work."

"If Ida doesn't want anyone around, why does she run an inn?" Phoebe asked, puzzled.

"She inherited the Yankee Bear free and clear when her husband, Joshua, died," Nathaniel explained. "The inn doesn't get a lot of business, but enough to pay the bills. Still, it is too bad Ida and Harriet can't move."

"Why can't they?" Phoebe asked.

"Ida's worked at the Yankee Bear since she married Joshua Thornwood forty-something years ago," Nathaniel said. "Running the inn is all she knows how to do. She's too old and too proud to work a service job for someone else."

"That's too bad," Phoebe said. "Going where no one knows about Harriet's affliction would be a good idea."

"That's not the reason Ida should leave," Nathaniel said. "Mystic Knoll is less than a quarter mile down the road. Getting away from it might cure Harriet."

"Seriously?" Blindsided by the extraordinary statement, Phoebe asked for clarification. "Are you saying that whatever drove a million bugs to kill themselves last night is causing Harriet's strange behavior?"

"You saw the swarm?" Nathaniel asked, surprised.

"Paige did," Phoebe explained.

Nathaniel leaned forward and rested his arms on his knees. "I don't buy into the local belief that Mystic Knoll has some kind of supernatural power."

"What *do* you think?" Phoebe asked.

"I think huge electromagnetic discharges affect the whole area," Nathaniel said, "some things more than others. Mostly—but not exclusively—wildlife . . . and Harriet."

Phoebe sat forward, struck again by the feeling that something was dreadfully wrong. "Why Harriet?"

"Proximity," Nathaniel said. "Except for old Jed's place, the Yankee Bear is the only residence within three miles of Mystic Knoll. It's possible that an entire lifetime of exposure made her highly susceptible to the surges."

"Is that Jed's problem too?" Phoebe asked.

Nathaniel shook his head. "He only moved in

a few years ago. Nobody lived there for years before that. Harriet has lived at the Yankee Bear since the day she was born."

"But overexposure to Mystic Knoll is only a theory," Phoebe said.

"Yeah, but it's the only explanation that makes sense." Standing up, Nathaniel took off his baseball cap, smoothed back his dark hair, and flipped the cap back on. "We'd better get back. I'm glad we talked, but don't tell Ida. She doesn't like people poking around in her business."

Phoebe smiled. "Yeah, I got that."

Harriet moaned when Nathaniel lifted her, but she didn't struggle. She rested her head on his shoulder as he led the way back to the inn.

The quiet walk through the forest helped Phoebe absorb everything they had discussed. Nathaniel's theory about electromagnetic emanations from Mystic Knoll was fascinating, but it wasn't the only explanation that made sense to a witch educated in psychology.

Was Ida protecting her granddaughter, as Nathaniel believed? Or was Harriet periodically giving in to an overwhelming sense of helplessness and acting out a lifelong fear of her grandmother?

"I can't believe they have three water goblets that match Grams's crystal," Piper whispered to Leo. They were huddled in a corner of an antique shop called Odds 'n' Ends, the third store they had browsed in the quaint New

England town. "And the price isn't that outrageous."

"They're thirty dollars apiece!" Leo hissed, keeping his voice low. Since the aisles were narrow and crammed with stuff, they had left the stroller by the front door. Wyatt had fallen asleep on Leo's shoulder.

"Trust me," Piper said as she carefully took the goblets off the shelf. "It's a bargain."

"Ten bucks." Leo rattled the small toy tractor and wagon he held in the hand cupped around Wyatt. "That's a bargain."

"Yes, dear." After giving him a quick peck on the cheek, Piper went to the front of the store and put the goblets on the counter. A thin, elderly man sat in a chair by the front window, reading a newspaper.

"Customer, Mabel!" the man called out without looking up.

"All right, Angus." A short, stocky woman came through a door in the wall behind the counter. "You don't have to shout."

"Do if your hearing aid's not turned on," Angus retorted. He tipped the chair back with the front legs off the floor, never taking his eyes from the paper.

Ignoring him, Mabel smiled at Piper. "Is this all?"

"And this." Leo rattled the tractor. Piper set it on the counter.

Mabel glanced at Wyatt and smiled. "Looks like

your little guy is too tuckered out to play with it."

"It's got lots of little metal pieces," Leo said. "I'm going to save it till he can appreciate it."

"Could you pack the goblets with extra padding?" Piper asked, handing the woman four twenties and a ten. "We're not going straight back to the inn."

"I can do better than that," Mabel said. "For an extra five dollars, I'll have them delivered. Where are you staying?"

"The Yankee Bear." Piper gave Mabel a five-dollar bill to cover the delivery charge.

"The Yankee Bear?" Mabel looked dismayed.

The legs of Angus's chair hit the floor with a crack. His eyes narrowed over the top edge of his paper. "Better get another twenty, Mabel."

"Another twenty?" Piper frowned, suddenly suspecting a scam. She wasn't about to be suckered by a crafty pair of old people trying to fleece the tourists. "What for?"

"To bribe the delivery boy," Angus huffed.

"Although I'm not sure extra money will convince Edgar to go out there," Mabel muttered.

"It's not that far," Leo said.

"No, but that's not the problem," Angus said. "Ida Thornwood doesn't like local folks coming around."

"It's not her fault," Mabel said as she wrapped the first goblet in protective bubble wrap. "Joshua was a hard man, and he kept poor Ida on a short leash when he was alive.

Twenty years and she never complained."

Piper assumed the deceased Joshua had been Ida's husband.

"Old habits die hard, I guess," Mabel said.

"Just like old rumors," Angus added pointedly.

Piper just nodded. Hearing the town gossip about the cranky innkeeper made her uncomfortable, but she didn't want to be rude. The old couple obviously enjoyed having an audience. Mabel was taking more time than she needed to wrap the goblets.

"Nobody ever proved Abigail bewitched her father into hanging himself, but the dang story just won't stay buried." Angus snorted with disgust.

"It never was buried," Mabel argued. She scowled at Angus, then turned back to Piper and Leo. She lowered her voice to a conspiratorial whisper. "There was bad blood between Abigail Thornwood and her father. Joshua refused to acknowledge she even existed, but nobody blamed him. Abigail was born deranged and marked by evil."

"Marked how?" Leo asked.

A moment earlier and Piper would have nudged him so he wouldn't encourage the gossiping. However, the mention of "evil" couldn't be ignored by a Whitelighter or a Charmed One.

"An ugly red blotch that covered almost half her face." Mabel held her hand at an angle across her right eye.

"A birthmark," Piper said.

Mabel nodded and carefully placed the second wrapped goblet in a small brown paper shopping bag with the first. "She was touched in the head to begin with and being the town outcast just made her madder. And I don't mean just angry."

"Beats me how she got in a family way with Harriet." Angus shook his head and turned the page of his newspaper.

"Abigail was only nineteen when she died having that girl," Mabel said. "Alone with her mother at the Yankee Bear. Harriet was never the trouble-maker her mother was, but she's just as crazy."

"And Ida?" Leo asked.

His interest troubled Piper. Was it idle curiosity, or did Leo detect something in the story that escaped her? A disfiguring birthmark and a dis-interested father who probably committed sui-cide were terrible burdens for a young girl, but nothing extraordinary in the magical sense.

"Ida takes care of her own, but nobody in Cairn goes out to the Yankee Bear without a good reason." Mabel put the third glass in the shopping bag and held out her hand for the extra cash for delivery.

"Thanks, but we'll take it." Piper picked up the bag and grabbed Leo's arm to haul him out of the store. He pulled back just long enough to grab the bag with the tractor and wagon.

"What's the big rush?" Leo asked when they were back outside. "They owe us five dollars."

"It was worth five bucks to get out of there."

Piper handed the goblet bag to Leo and took Wyatt. He woke up when she put him back in the stroller. "I really didn't need to hear Ida and Harriet's tragic life histories."

"They've obviously had a hard time," Leo said.

"That's probably why the whole conversation creeped me out." Piper shuddered.

Leo was ever the sympathetic soul, but she was on vacation and in no mood to let anything spoil the day, especially a problem no one had asked them to solve.

"I thought Mabel and Angus were a hoot," Leo said.

"A hoot?" Piper rolled her eyes at the outdated expression. Leo winced when Wyatt started to howl. He gave the bags back to Piper and grabbed the stroller push bar.

"C'mon, big guy," he said to his son. "It's time to go have some fun!"

The movement of the rolling stroller calmed Wyatt down. He was dry eyed and quiet when they arrived at the park. On a side street across from a brick school, the grassy expanse was equipped with swings, a push-go-round, teeter-totters, and elaborate climbing structures. Large oaks and maples shaded picnic tables and a triple-tiered water fountain. Piper sat on the ground, watching while Leo pushed Wyatt in a baby swing.

"Not too high, Dad," Piper admonished Leo.

"Don't worry." Leo laughed when Wyatt squealed. "He likes it."

Piper lay back to stare at wisps of white cloud in the blue sky. She had to remember to thank Paige for pushing the vacation idea. Lying on the grass listening to her husband and son laugh was the first time in ages she had felt that all was right with the world.

Then a fat brown toad jumped on her chest.

"Ahhh!" Startled, Piper swatted the creature away as she jumped to her feet.

"What?" Leo stopped Wyatt's swing with a frantic look in her direction.

"Nothing." Piper shrugged, feeling a little foolish. "Just a toad with no sense of direction."

"Uh-guh!" Gurgling, Wyatt waved his hands.

"It's more than just a toad," Leo said as screams erupted around them.

Following Leo's gaze, Piper turned and stared as mothers grabbed kids off jungle gyms, swing sets, and picnic table benches. They ran for the parking lot, leaving diaper bags, picnic baskets, strollers, and tricycles.

Wyatt laughed as thousands of toads emerged from hiding under rocks and in the grass, transforming the park into an undulating sea of brown amphibians.

Chapter
4

Phoebe had returned to the wooden lawn chair when Nathaniel took Harriet back into the house. Ida's truck was parked by a large equipment shed behind the inn. With the old woman there to take care of the runaway, Phoebe didn't worry when Nathaniel walked down the long driveway with a Weed Eater a few minutes later. She settled back to read.

Phantom Fire had started to pick up, but she couldn't concentrate on the intricate plot. Her mind kept wandering back to her earlier conversation with Nathaniel.

She had no reason to doubt that Harriet experienced uncontrollable bursts of odd behavior. The question nagging at her was what caused them.

Ordinarily, eliminating a physical problem would leave two other options as the cause of Harriet's condition: emotional or supernatural.

This time, however, Phoebe had to consider the effects of electromagnetic discharges as well. The scientific theory was as plausible as the possibility that Mystic Knoll exerted some kind of mystical power over the community.

Plausible from a witch's perspective anyway, Phoebe thought.

She opened her eyes and pulled the Mystic Knoll brochure out of the paperback. The cover photograph depicted a large monolithic boulder with a crude notch chiseled into the top. Sunlight glinted through the notch. According to the brochure, carbon-dating of pottery shards and bone tools found at the archaeological dig site indicated that the stone structures were four thousand years old.

Phoebe unfolded the pamphlet and glanced over the color photographs inside. Primitive monoliths guarded meandering stone walkways overgrown with vines and moss. A network of open passageways and underground tunnels connected several subterranean chambers. A diagram showed that the pattern was random, with the largest cavern off center, near the north side. According to the text, the stone configuration had served as a fortification or an astronomical device.

"Except that something about it probably makes the local wildlife go crazy," Phoebe mumbled to herself.

Myths and legends did not evolve without

having some basis in reality. The problem, Phoebe realized, was that *either* magic or electromagnetic energy could explain Mystic Knoll's unusual properties. She had more questions for Nathaniel, but he was weeding the gardens by the road, and she didn't want to raise any suspicions.

Phoebe put the brochure back in her book and leaned back. She closed her eyes and became aware of a noise rising behind her that had not been audible a moment before. It reminded her of a playing card snapping against the spokes of a spinning bicycle wheel. She sat up, glanced back, and immediately rolled off the chair to lie flat on the ground, covering her head.

It was a scene right out of the old Alfred Hitchcock movie *The Birds*. Phoebe cringed as hundreds of brown sparrows flew by. Unlike the squawking, screeching crows in the movie, these birds were silent except for their beating wings. Flying at low altitude, a few collided with the back of the lawn chair. Breaking necks or stunning themselves, the small birds fell in the grass around her.

Phoebe waited a moment more after the last few stragglers in the massive flock had passed. Then she stood up cautiously, her gaze locked on the dark cloud that swept across the lawn toward the three-story house.

Are the birds on the same suicidal course as the bugs Paige saw last night? Phoebe wondered.

She tensed, as the frenzied swarm suddenly turned upward instead of flying into the side of the inn. Moving as a single entity, they swooped up the wall and across the shingled roof. At the roof's peak, the birds went into another vertical climb, then reversed direction and dove into the redbrick chimney.

"What on earth?" Phoebe rubbed her eyes. She had seen too many weird, disturbing things to be totally shocked, but the mob of crazed sparrows was particularly unsettling because the small birds were usually so innocuous. *Or should be*, she thought.

Picking up her book and towel, Phoebe hesitated before starting back to the house.

Was the chimney filling up with berserk sparrows or were the birds spilling out of the kitchen fireplace? Vivid pictures flashed into Phoebe's mind. She imagined a feathered tornado circling the butcher-block island, picking up speed, and flinging off the slow and weak. Dozens might be smashing into walls and windows, banging into hanging pots, and dropping into heaps on the floor.

A high-pitched shriek blotted the disturbing pictures from Phoebe's thoughts. A moment later Harriet ran out the front door. The young woman raced down the porch steps and across the lawn, screaming and waving her arms to ward off the birds streaming behind her.

"Harriet!" Brandishing a broom, Ida stormed out the door behind her. Limited by age, she raced after her granddaughter in a hobbling half stride that was not quite a run.

Reacting on instinct, Phoebe bolted toward Harriet. When she was halfway across the lawn, the flock suddenly broke off the attack and dispersed. Surprised and confused, Phoebe slowed back to a walk.

As the birds flew into the sky or nearby trees, Harriet collapsed with trembling sobs.

Ida dropped her broom and kneeled on the ground beside the stricken woman.

"Is everything okay?" Phoebe asked as she drew near.

Ida looked up sharply and motioned her to stay back. "She will be. Just leave her alone."

Phoebe stopped a few feet away. "Sure. I was just worried—"

"I'll handle it," Ida snapped, drawing Harriet close. The young woman's shoulders shook as she buried her face in her grandmother's lap. "Go away."

Nodding, Phoebe slung her towel over her shoulder and turned toward the house. She hoped she wouldn't have to navigate through too many dead birds to get to her room, but that was a stray thought. Her mind was trying to grasp the larger implications.

Whether scientific or paranormal forces were at work, something strange was going on. Phoebe couldn't shake the perception that the birds had deliberately entered the house to go after Harriet.

• • •

Paige spent a few minutes wandering the roped-off paths through the Mystic Knoll archaeological dig, but the most interesting artifacts had been removed. With ten minutes left before the tour started, she abandoned the dig to go back into the gift shop.

A sign in the window informed the public that Cairn Township used the money collected from tours and gift shop sales to operate and maintain the site. The Mystic Knoll logo was designed with the two angled lines of the "K" attached to the "M" to form MK over a stylized rock slab. The design was burned into a wooden plaque over the door with the words MYSTIC KNOLL, EST. CIRCA 2000 BC. The ancient date made Paige laugh as she pulled open the screen door.

"We'll get started in a few minutes." The woman behind the front counter spoke to Paige as she ambled by.

"Thanks, Tammy. I'm not in a hurry," Paige said, smiling. She had met Tammy when she purchased her tour ticket.

Tammy was forty, with short, graying hair and the weathered face of an outdoors person. She wore jeans and a hunter green T-shirt with the Mystic Knoll logo, address, and phone number on the back. She was making change for a silver-haired couple.

"We got here just in time, Doreen." The man slipped his wallet into the back pocket of his Bermuda-style shorts.

"Will we be done in time to make the lunch special at Gorman's?" Doreen asked Tammy. "It's fried shrimp today."

"Yes, plenty of time," Tammy said.

"Excellent," the man said. "We've been wanting to take this tour for years and never got around to it."

"It's just a bunch of rocks, Larry." Doreen shook her head, a gesture that betrayed her true feelings about the tour. She had no interest in Mystic Knoll beyond minimal tolerance for her husband's enthusiasm.

Paige exchanged an amused glance with Tammy and pointed toward the book aisle. "I'll be over here."

Paige had questions for Tammy, but she hesitated to ask in front of an audience. There were no piles of dead bugs around the Mystic Knoll gift shop, which was only a quarter mile from the Yankee Bear. Had the swarms missed the secluded building, or had Tammy cleaned up and disposed of the bodies? Answers would have to wait until after the tour, when she could talk to the guide alone.

Paige browsed the bookshelves. Only two of the volumes dealt specifically with the Mystic Knoll antiquity. One was a more detailed map of the site and the other an expanded version of the brochure. Paige decided to wait until after the tour to make a purchase. Most of the other books were on related subjects, such as Stonehenge in

Britain, the local Native American tribes, New England histories, and New Hampshire tourist spots.

When Tammy called the tour group outside a few minutes later, another couple joined Paige, Doreen, and Larry. Joyce and Daniel were newlyweds in their late twenties. They were cruising the back roads of America in a rented RV, stopping at points of interest they encountered along the way. After giving everyone a large flashlight, Tammy led the way down a path cushioned with pine needles.

Paige brought up the rear, enjoying the hike through the stillness of the woods. Sunlight filtered through the overhead foliage and glistened off wild toadstools and ferns on the forest floor. Squirrels scampered up and down tree trunks, and birds flitted through blackberry briars. Bees and butterflies drank at wildflower fountains, reminding Paige of her brief sojourn as a wood nymph. The almost pristine quality of this woodland showed how much the sprites favored it.

Tammy stopped the group by a large boulder with a circular base. The top of the rock had been chipped into a flat surface at an oblique angle. The front edge was eighteen inches off the ground, rising to four feet high in the back. The guide waited until everyone had a chance to examine the stone before starting her spiel.

"Despite the structural differences," Tammy began, "Britain's Stonehenge and Mystic Knoll are accurate astronomical calendars that mark solar and lunar events."

"Like the solar eclipse this Sunday?" Paige asked, recalling Nathaniel's argument for why Ida should keep the Yankee Bear open.

"Not quite that precise," Tammy said. "The stones were positioned to align with sunrises and sunsets during the spring and fall equinoxes and the summer and winter solstices."

"Will someone take our picture by that rock?" Joyce asked.

"Monolith," Tammy corrected. "This one is the summer solstice sunrise stone."

"Whatever." Joyce handed Paige a disposable camera. "Would you? I'm keeping a scrapbook journal of our honeymoon adventures."

"Whatever." Paige resented the young's woman's rude, self-centered attitude, but it wasn't worth an argument. She took the camera and snapped a couple of shots of Joyce and Daniel posing on the angled rock.

Doreen watched with wistful approval, but her husband, Larry, looked annoyed, as though the young lovers had desecrated the pagan stone. When Joyce and Daniel jumped down, he wiped off the smooth surface.

"Thanks." Joyce took the camera back and clasped Daniel's hand as they continued down the path.

The trees grew larger and closer together the deeper they walked into the woods. Fewer rays of sunlight penetrated the dense canopy of leaves, and the temperature dropped a few chilling degrees. Paige shivered, but she wasn't sure if the sensation was real or an imagined manifestation created by the darkening shadows. The chill did not dissipate when everyone halted at the edge of the Mystic Knoll clearing.

"Oh, my." Doreen paused with her hand at her throat, scanning the expansive collection of stone huts, bridges, walls, and monoliths.

"Told you it would be impressive, Doreen." Vindicated, Larry smiled, crossed his arms, and rocked back on his heels. "But this is even better than I imagined."

"What did they do here?" Joyce asked.

"Who were they?" Daniel added.

"That's the subject of much debate," Tammy explained as she led them along a twisting stone path. "This may have been the village of a primitive tribe. They may have been the ancestors of the Iroquois who claimed this territory five hundred years ago. They, of course, were driven west by the European settlers."

Paige kept to the rear, taking in every detail of the ancient stone artifacts. The clearing was not completely devoid of trees. The sun warmed and dried the open spaces, but where water seeped between stones in the shadows, the damp was tangible. A stream cut through the center of the clearing, bubbling over rocks, between huts, and under a footbridge that was clearly built for tourists.

"Sit on that stone bench over there, Daniel." Joyce pointed to a large slab. Stacked rocks at the four corners raised the massive flat stone eighteen inches off the ground.

Daniel jumped to obey as his new wife raised the camera.

"Looks like a sacrificial stone to me," Paige said as Daniel started to sit. He jumped up, inhaling sharply.

"Most of the experts agree that rituals of some sort were conducted on the site," Tammy said. "But only the people who live around here think Mystic Knoll is cursed."

"*I* don't believe that rubbish," Doreen said.

Tammy ignored the comment. "Some even think the town is cursed too."

Joyce and Daniel exchanged a nervous glance.

There wasn't a hint of a smile in Tammy's somber expression as she loaded the young couple's susceptible minds with the creepy local legend.

Unless she isn't kidding, Paige thought.

"Who cursed it?" Paige asked.

"A Native American shaman?" Tammy shrugged. "A witch? There's a lot of local speculation about that, too."

The hair on Paige's neck prickled. She hadn't expected a reference to witches. However, Wiccan beliefs shared many basic precepts with Druidic disciplines and Native American lore.

They each embraced a natural order infused with a universal spirituality that was akin to magic. Stonehenge in Britain was believed to be Druidic. Was Mystic Knoll a combination of all three cultures?

"What kind of curse?" Paige asked.

"I don't think I want to know." Joyce gripped Daniel's arm and pressed close to her husband.

"There's no such thing as curses," Daniel said, closing his large hand over Joyce's smaller one.

"Or witches," Larry said. "Maybe some grisly ghost with a grudge haunts the place," he added sarcastically.

"Not that I'm aware of," Tammy said.

"What about swarms of bugs bashing barns in the middle of the night?" Paige asked, baiting Tammy.

Tammy just shrugged. "Things like that happen around here, but the incidents can be explained scientifically."

"How?" Paige pressed.

"The latest theory has something to do with electromagnetic energy." Tammy abruptly changed the subject. "Now, if you'll all follow me—"

Paige kept her place at the end of the line and stooped to enter one of the low stone chambers. Tammy had given her food for thought, but nothing she could sink her teeth into. She couldn't tell if the guide gave credence to curses or was just selling the story to drum up business.

She put the questions aside to focus more carefully on her step when the floor sloped downward at a steep angle. The interior ambience of Mystic Knoll was even creepier than the deep woods and abandoned stone huts in the clearing. The rock walls were damp and covered with moss. Rotting leaves had collected in cracks and crevices, tainting the air with the odor of compost.

Paige tried to picture the diagram in the brochure, but she couldn't orient their location until they emerged into the main chamber. The huge cave was natural and had been incorporated into the ancient building plan. Everyone panned their flashlight beams around the cavern, but it was impossible to grasp the magnificence of the immense grotto in the diffuse light.

"Okay, everyone," Tammy said, clapping her hands for attention. "Turn off your flashlights."

"Seriously?" Joyce asked uncertainly.

"I'm right here, honey bunch," Daniel said. "There's nothing to worry about."

"Honey bunch," Larry scoffed, turning off his flashlight. "He sounds like a walking romance novel."

"Hush up," Doreen retorted.

The other flashlights clicked off, but the group was not enveloped in darkness. The walls glowed brighter as each light was extinguished.

"Oh, my!" Doreen gasped again.

"Told you this would be worth the time," Larry said.

"Wow!" Joyce stared at the golden luminescence on the rock around them.

"Phosphorescent lichen," Tammy explained. "It's similar to fox fire, another variety of glowing plant that grows on decaying trees in the Appalachians."

"It's beautiful." Paige was impressed. Despite the magical marvels she had seen since becoming a Charmed One, nothing was quite as awe inspiring as a natural wonder.

The light source revealed the irregular, amoeba-like shape of the cavern. The perimeter wall was riddled with dark crevices and alcoves, and the high ceiling was covered with stalactites. The inverted cones were accumulated mineral deposits created over eons by dripping water. Most of the corresponding stalagmites on the central portion of floor had been removed. Three large cones remained, spaced at equal intervals around another raised slab of flat rock.

"What went on down here?" Daniel asked.

"No one knows, but this part of the site has nothing to do with astronomy." Tammy pointed up. "No view of the sky."

After fielding a few more questions, Tammy took the tour out through a different tunnel.

Paige wasn't sorry she had come. The glowing cavern was worth the price of the tour, but she hadn't learned anything that might explain the house-battering bugs . . . or why Harriet might have battered herself on her bedroom wall.

"Fresh air!" Joyce inhaled deeply when they reached a section of corridor that was open to the sky.

Paige realized that the piles of rock on either side of the passageway were the remains of the ceiling. At some point during the past four thousand years, the roof had caved in.

Joyce perched on a large rock halfway up the pile. "Give the camera to someone and c'mon up, Danny. This will make a great shot."

"Larry's turn," Paige said when Daniel held out the camera. She had already made her contribution to Joyce's honeymoon digest, and she didn't want the distraction.

The tour was almost over, and Paige couldn't decide if she wanted to approach Tammy for more information. Nobody talked about real curses in public. Besides, she hadn't seen anything on the tour that supported a paranormal reason for the insect incident. If electromagnetism was responsible, it didn't seem likely that Tammy had the scientific expertise to explain it.

"Danny! Stop." Joyce squealed and leaned closer to her husband. She lowered her voice, her expression coy. "Can't you wait until we get back to the RV?"

"Wait for what?" Danny looked perplexed.

"Was I ever that dense?" Larry asked Doreen.

"No, dear." Doreen smiled and patted his arm.

Paige covered her mouth to hide a smile.

"Stop that!" Joyce giggled and shifted position

on the rock. She raised her hand to cuff Daniel's shoulder and stiffened. "Your hands are in your lap."

"Yeah, so?" Danny frowned, puzzled.

"So—" Joyce screamed when a small black and yellow snake slithered across her lap. She stood up, dumping the hapless creature on the rock floor. As it escaped into the rocks, she jumped up and down, shrieking. "Ooh, gross. I can't stand snakes!"

"It's all right, sweetie." Daniel put his arms around his hysterical wife. "It was just a harmless little garter snake."

"There's another one!" Larry pointed at Daniel's feet. "And another one!"

Paige wasn't big on snakes either, which made their present location a really bad place to be. The passageway was suddenly oozing snakes.

"Ahh! Ahh!" Doreen shifted from one foot to another to avoid a mass of wiggling green, yellow, and black snakes. She was terrified and fell into Larry's arms.

"Okay, dear. Time to go." Larry slung Doreen's arm over his shoulder and helped her stumble forward. He started into the next tunnel and stopped dead. "I hope there's another way back."

"Me too." Paige shone her flashlight inside the narrow stone corridor. The passage floor was covered with snakes. Several began shedding their skins.

"Cross-country," Tammy said, taking charge.

Ignoring the snakes sliding out of the rock pile, she climbed it. "This way."

Paige let Joyce and Daniel go first, then steadied Larry as he carried Doreen up the rock pile. When Paige reached the top, she realized that cutting through the woods was only a slightly better alternative than taking the tunnels.

The ground was alive with thousands of writhing snakes.

"I'm not convinced it was Wyatt," Leo said. He smiled as he offered his son another spoonful of ice cream.

Piper just looked at her husband. They had taken refuge in the Parfait Café, hoping ice cream would take Wyatt's mind off his little brown friends. Since several thousand toads weren't breaking down the door to reach him, she assumed the distraction had worked.

"One or two toads, maybe," Leo muttered.

"He was fascinated by Phoebe's frog salt and pepper shakers," Piper mused. "And they are brown—like toads."

"You think salt and pepper shakers inspired him?" Leo sounded skeptical.

"He brought his tub toys and a cartoon dog to life," Piper said, lowering her voice. "Why wouldn't he call every toad in town out to play?"

"Maybe that's not the right question." Leo wiped Wyatt's mouth. "Maybe we should be asking, why would he?"

That's actually a good question, Piper thought. Except for raising his force field to protect himself, Wyatt didn't use his powers often. They didn't know what triggered his desire to use magic.

"Maybe he was bored," Piper said. She took a sip of coffee, but it was getting cold. She swallowed with a grimace and set the cup down.

"Bored swinging?" Leo's tone was skeptical. He shook his head. "No way. Swinging is one of Wyatt's favorite things to do."

Piper sighed, stumped. Until today they had been lucky—Wyatt hadn't created any public displays of power. She hated the idea of having to hide out for fear he'd do something they couldn't explain away.

"Wait a minute." Piper sat back. "The park was just overrun with toads. How come nobody's upset?"

Leo shrugged. "Maybe the town has a chronic toad problem?"

"Maybe we should ask." Piper raised her arm to get the waitress's attention.

"How's everything going here?" the pretty, twenty-something waitress asked, smiling.

"Fine," Piper said, noting the name tag. "Lucy, could I have a warm-up?"

"Sure. Do you want a clean cup?" Lucy asked.

"Not necessary." Piper waited until the coffee was poured before bringing up toads. As she started to speak, the black liquid in her cup started to boil. "Uh, that's a little too hot, isn't it?"

Leo nudged her knee and pointed to his half-empty cup. His coffee was boiling too. He quickly scooped more ice cream onto the spoon. "Hey, Wyatt! Ice cream."

Piper noticed that the coffee inside Lucy's glass pot was bubbling, but she was pretty sure Wyatt wasn't to blame. He had no idea what "warm-up" meant, and he was totally into his ice cream at the moment.

"Well, this could be worse." A man at the next table threw up his hands. "Lucy, could I have an ice cube?"

"Right away, Mr. Farley." Lucy hurried back to the counter.

Leo and Piper exchanged a confused glance.

"No, no!" A woman at the table behind Leo knocked her chair over as she stood up. Her blond hair was too blond to be natural, and her jeans were too snug to be comfortable. She was forty but determined to look twenty-nine as long as possible. "No, no, no!"

"It's all right, Gretchen," Mr. Farley said. "Just a little hot coffee. Nothing to worry about."

Gretchen apparently didn't agree. The woman burst into tears and ran into the ladies' room.

When no one moved for a moment, Piper leaned toward Mr. Farley's table. "Should someone go after her?"

"Nah." Mr. Farley shook his head. "Just an anxiety attack. She'll get over it. Gretchen hasn't been quite right since her teeth turned black when she was sixteen."

"That's enough, Mr. Farley," Lucy chided the man. She dropped an ice cube into his coffee cup. "You know Gretchen's still sensitive about that."

"How could such a thing happen?" Leo spooned more ice cream into Wyatt.

"Happened overnight," Mr. Farley said. He leaned toward Leo. "But I don't believe for a minute that Abigail Thornwood used some kind of mumbo jumbo to get even with Gretchen for making fun of her at cheerleading tryouts."

"You spread more tall tales than an old woman, Mr. Farley," Lucy scolded.

"They're not tales if they're true," the man shot back with a triumphant smile.

Leo cast another quizzical glance at Piper.

Piper smiled tightly. She didn't know what kind, but some kind of mumbo jumbo was definitely in play.

All the coffee in the café had boiled for no apparent reason.

And everyone except Gretchen had acted like it was no big deal.

Chapter
5

Phoebe paced in the front foyer of the Yankee Bear, wondering what to do about Harriet. She never questioned her Charmed right to act when the danger was supernatural. The decision wasn't that simple when the situation fell entirely within the realm of human endeavor.

Phoebe had watched from the landing as Ida guided her distraught granddaughter into the house after the sparrow attack. Harriet hadn't said a word, but the helpless misery she felt was evident in every labored breath and shuffling step. Even when the two women were out of sight, Harriet's despair was like a heavy, inescapable haze permeating the inn.

Although everything about the young woman's situation cried out for help, Harriet hadn't asked for any.

Phoebe's indecision evaporated when a keening wail rose from the back of the house.

"That's it." Phoebe started down the hall, taking care to maintain a calm exterior, and paused at the junction of the second hallway. Straight ahead, the door into the kitchen was closed. Honing in on the fading wail, she turned down the second hall. The left-hand wall partitioned the narrow passageway from the area behind the registration counter in the foyer. She heard muted sobs coming through the second of three doors on the right.

Taking a deep breath, Phoebe grabbed the knob. The sound of Ida's gruff voice stopped her from barging in.

"Calm down, girl," Ida said. "I'll get some lotion. You'll be fine."

Phoebe took a startled step back when Ida pulled the door open. Pain and fear washed over her like a wave, drawing her gaze past Ida's slim frame.

Harriet sat crossed-legged on the floor, rocking back and forth. Long strips of dry skin were peeling off her hands, face, and arms . . . but she was not sunburned.

Ida took a key from her pocket and forced Phoebe back another step as she moved into the hall. She closed the door and turned to lock it.

"What are you doing snooping about?" Ida asked, turning back to face Phoebe.

"I was worried about Harriet," Phoebe honestly answered, her voice even. "Paige told me she has nightmares. After what happened with the birds, I thought maybe I could help. I'm a psychologist."

"Harriet doesn't need a psychologist." Ida spat out the word. "She has fits sometimes, like you saw today. Messing with the poor child's head won't fix it."

"Are you sure?" Phoebe asked, standing her ground.

"Yes." Ida glared at Phoebe.

Phoebe had already determined that Ida wouldn't back down if cornered or challenged. The old woman used cantankerous bluster to keep people at bay. Most of the Yankee Bear guests probably liked the crusty New England persona Ida presented. Harriet's plain appearance and bumbling behavior no doubt repelled them, which helped Ida enforce Harriet's isolation.

Phoebe, however, was not a typical guest.

"Why is her skin peeling?" Phoebe asked.

"Allergies," Ida said without hesitation. "I've got to get her medicine—if you'll get out of my way."

Since Harriet's sobs had stopped and Ida's explanations matched what Nathaniel had told her earlier, Phoebe decided to back off. *For now,* she thought as Ida impatiently motioned her to move.

"This area is off limits to guests too," Ida said as she bustled behind Phoebe to the kitchen hall. "Besides, it's long past checkout time."

"We'd like to stay another night," Phoebe said. In fairness, she couldn't hide their plans from Ida any longer.

Ida frowned. "You said you'd only be staying one night."

"I know, but something came up." Phoebe shrugged. For a moment, she thought Ida was going to argue. Instead the old woman turned toward the kitchen.

"Checkout time is two o'clock and not a minute later." Ida opened the door into the kitchen and looked back before closing it behind her. "Tomorrow."

We'll see, Phoebe thought. She wasn't leaving until she was certain Harriet wasn't in danger— from her grandmother or herself.

"You don't have to do this," Tammy said as she unlocked the gift shop door and threw it open.

"I'm not leaving you here alone to close up," Paige said. She jumped over a tangled mass of snakes on the steps, landed on the front stoop with one foot, and put her other foot down inside the shop. She grabbed the door to steady herself and looked back at the serpentine knot with a shudder. She pulled the screen door closed and latched it.

"I don't think they can get in here," Tammy said. She walked up and down the aisles to make sure.

Through the screen, Paige watched Larry and Daniel dart, bob, and hop around piles of snakes to the dirt parking area. They were both helping their wives run, which made eluding the serpents harder.

The group had made the harrowing run through the woods harder on her. Being in human company prevented her from orbing the snakes to clear a path. An infestation of shedding snakes was beyond strange but still within the bounds of possibility in a town that thought nothing of thousands of kamikaze bugs. Snakes disappearing in swirls of blue light was not.

Forced to rely on her nonmagical abilities, Paige had developed a fairly proficient means of snake avoidance. The trick was to not hesitate leaping from one rock, downed tree, or rare snake-free spot to another. The realization that the creatures were immobilized or slowed down during the process of losing their skins had helped.

"All clear." Tammy paused beside Paige as Daniel and Larry drove away. "Where's your car?"

"I walked from the Yankee Bear," Paige explained. She patted the cell phone clipped to her belt. "I'll call my sister for a ride."

"Most cell phones don't work around here," Tammy said. "We're too far from the city."

"Oh. Well, that's okay," Paige said. "If I run into any stray snakes, they won't bother me."

"I don't want to leave you with the wrong

impression of Mystic Knoll," Tammy said. "I'll give you a ride. I just need a few minutes to fill out the bank deposit."

"Great." Paige followed Tammy to the counter. "How often do you have to close down because of snakes?"

"This is the first time," Tammy said. The old-fashioned mechanical cash register *dinged* when she opened the drawer. She pulled out the one-dollar bills and started counting.

Paige nodded, but Tammy's matter-of-fact tone surprised her. She had assumed the guide stayed calm about the snakes to avoid total panic in the tour group. She hadn't expected Tammy's unruffled acceptance of the bizarre event to persist.

"First time for *snakes*, that is." Tammy set the one-dollar bills aside and wrote the amount in a ledger. "Poison ivy shut us down for a few days three months ago."

"Did we run through any today?" Paige asked, choking back a gasp. She did not want her vacation ruined by an itchy rash.

"No." Tammy began counting fives and paused. "That was pretty weird too. One morning the whole site was overgrown with poison ivy vines, and four days later they were all gone."

"Huh?" Relieved, Paige kept the conversation going. "So this kind of thing happens a lot, then."

"Every once in a while." Tammy finished

counting out the fives, then frowned. "Although I don't remember as much stuff happening when I was a kid."

"Like swarms of suicidal bugs?" Paige asked.

"Bugs fly into stuff all the time," Tammy said. "That's just how bugs are." She took two tens and four twenties from the drawer and noted the amounts.

Paige let the subject drop, realizing that Tammy hadn't encountered millions of berserk bugs.

"But," Tammy continued, "we haven't had anything as freaky as the snakes happen since all the squirrels in town went on a rampage when I was nineteen."

"Squirrels?" Paige asked, confused. "The cute little furry kind?"

"Believe me, they aren't cute when they're leaping off trees to yank out your hair." Tammy grimaced as she stuffed the bills into a green deposit bag. "That was twenty years ago, and I still get chills thinking about it."

"I can imagine," Paige said. "Does anybody know why these weird things happen?"

"Not really." Tammy locked the coins in the drawer. "Almost everyone in town thinks Mystic Knoll gives off some kind of electrical energy that affects the natural order, but most of them won't admit it."

"Why not?" Paige asked. At first she was surprised. Then she remembered something Nathaniel had said the night before. . . . *Most people completely reject scientific explanations that shatter their myths. . . . Half the folks in Cairn think Mystic Knoll has some kind of weird power.*

"Because a curse is better for business," Tammy explained. "Except I'm pretty sure Abigail Thornwood *did* put a hex on the town."

"Thornwood?" Paige frowned. "The same Thornwoods who own the Yankee Bear?"

Tammy nodded. "Ida's daughter. She died having Harriet . . . *before* she removed the hex."

"Do you really believe that?" Paige asked, feigning the rational skepticism a normal person would express.

"Absolutely." Tammy leaned over the counter. "I was a year behind Abigail in school. She made Karen Stark's hair fall out in seventh grade."

"Abigail did? Why?"

"Because Karen called her a mutant. Bad stuff happened to everyone who gave Abigail a hard time. Karen was bald for six months." Tammy zipped the deposit bag and retrieved her purse from under the counter. "Ready?"

Paige nodded and followed Tammy out. She ran every tidbit of information over in her mind, carefully locking it into her memory. She had learned much more at Mystic Knoll than she had anticipated, and the various factors—freaked-out wildlife, a possible witch, and the undefined power of Mystic Knoll—were beginning to add up to a Charmed encounter.

• • •

"How long is the wait?" Phoebe asked when Leo came back to the patio from the hostess station. The tantalizing aromas emanating from the restaurant made the delay torturous. She hadn't eaten since breakfast, and she was famished.

After everyone had returned to the inn that afternoon, they decided to grab an early dinner in town. They were all hungry, and Phoebe wanted to discuss the day's events away from potential prying eyes and ears at the Yankee Bear.

On the ride into Cairn, Phoebe realized that she wasn't the only one who had had an unsettling brush with crazed wildlife and Ida Thornwood. Her sisters had both heard gossip about the Thornwood family and witnessed bizarre behavior on their side trips into town and Mystic Knoll.

"Ten minutes," Leo said, sitting down at the table in the outdoor lounge. "Apparently Nathaniel picked one of the most popular spots in town for his dinner date with Paige."

Paige's face creased in a playful scowl. "Yeah, but somehow I don't think Nathaniel thought the whole family would tag along as chaperones."

"We're not going to sit at the same table," Piper teased. She set down her iced-tea glass and lifted Wyatt out of his stroller when he began to fuss. "Besides, I couldn't resist eating at a place called 'Fish, Fowl, and Cow.'"

"That covers all the bases I care about." Leo jangled his car keys to amuse Wyatt. Wyatt batted his father's hand away and rubbed his eyes.

"Are we sure the n-e-p-h-e-w didn't start the t-o-a-d riot?" Paige asked, leaning toward Piper and whispering.

"Positive," Piper whispered back. "The b-a-b-y wasn't around when the b-u-g-s and the s-n-a-k-e-s went all wild and weird, remember?"

"Don't forget the b-i-r-d-s," Phoebe added. She didn't think they needed to spell in front of Wyatt yet, but the practice couldn't hurt.

"Good point," Paige said. "So why am I not more relieved?"

"Maybe because our vacation is starting to feel like a mission?" Phoebe smiled, but she wasn't kidding. "What else did you learn about Mystic Knoll?"

"Well, the site might have been a fort or a village, and it's set up as an astronomical calendar," Paige said. "The original inhabitants either died out or evolved into a Native American tribe of the Iroquois."

"There's another possibility you won't find in the tourist literature," Leo said.

Piper perked up. "Is Daddy going to tell a story?"

Responding to the word "daddy," Wyatt leaned against Piper and looked at Leo.

"Your mommy is so smart." Leo smiled at

Wyatt and spoke with a storybook cadence and inflection. "A long, long time ago in Ireland, there were magic people called the 'Tuatha de Danann.'"

"Ooh, cool." Paige reacted for Wyatt's benefit.

"In fact," Leo went on, "it wasn't even called Ireland yet! But that's another story."

Piper spoke through a tight smile. "Let's just get on with this one."

"Don't cramp my style." Leo turned back to Wyatt. In his story-telling voice, he continued. "The ancient Celts believed that the magic people *flew* to Ireland from the *west* several thousand years ago."

"Several, as in four?" Paige held up four fingers.

"Flew through the sky?" Phoebe asked.

"From *this* west?" Piper pointed at the ground, meaning New Hampshire.

Leo nodded. "Maybe the magic people built Mystic Knoll before they left."

"Maybe they left because there aren't any snakes in Ireland," Paige muttered.

"He's asleep," Phoebe said, pointing at Wyatt.

"Good." Piper clamped her arms around the dozing boy and swayed gently from side to side.

"The end," Leo said softly.

"A nice story, Leo," Paige said, "but it doesn't explain why thousands of snakes decided to shed skin at Mystic Knoll. The locals think the place is cursed or an electromagnetic force."

"The bugs and the birds attacked the Yankee Bear," Piper said.

"Come to think of it, though," Phoebe said, "Harriet's skin peeled at the same time the snakes were shedding."

"And she was bashing her bedroom wall when the bugs hit the house," Paige added.

"So maybe the birds didn't attack her," Phoebe mused, thinking out loud. "Maybe Harriet had one of her fits at the same time the birds wigged out."

"Could electromagnetic energy account for that?" Paige asked.

"Nathaniel thinks Harriet is supersensitive to the discharges because she's lived so close to Mystic Knoll her whole life," Phoebe explained.

"I suppose that's possible," Paige said.

Piper flipped a lever to recline the stroller and carefully lay Wyatt down. As she straightened up, her iced-tea spoon flipped on end, zoomed off the table, and stuck to the metal handle on the stroller.

"Hello?" Piper scowled. "What just happened?"

"Uh—" Phoebe winced. The pendant on her necklace stood straight out from her neck, straining away from her. "I think all the metal on the patio just became magnetized."

"You think?" Paige jumped when several loose dimes zeroed in on her earrings.

At the surrounding tables, metal caps on salt

and pepper shakers wobbled and rolled, attracted to metal watch bands and handbag clasps. A woman walking on to the patio from the restaurant stopped short when her bracelet latched onto her child's braces.

"Interesting," Leo said as he tried to pry a paper clip off his belt buckle.

"For a science whiz maybe." Paige flicked the dimes attached to her earrings.

Piper's wedding ring was stuck to the metal button on her charcoal gray slacks. A butter knife zooming toward Wyatt's stroller bounced off his protective shield.

Then, all of a sudden, the displaced items disengaged and fell.

"Finders keepers," Paige said, scooping up the dimes on the table. "I guess this little demonstration supports the scientific theory."

"The effects seem too random to be a spell," Leo said. "And curses are almost always specific."

"But we can't rule out that something supernatural might be operating in the area," Phoebe said.

"I can't," Piper agreed. "Electromagnetism doesn't explain the boiling coffee at the café this afternoon."

"It could if the discharges affected the electric coffeemakers." Leo shrugged.

"The coffee in Lucy's pot and our cups boiled too," Piper argued. "No coffeemakers involved."

"There's Nathaniel," Paige said. She stood

up and waved at her date. "See you later."

"Have fun," Piper said, waving her away.

Phoebe smiled too, but her mind was on Mystic Knoll and the day's strange events. She *wanted* the source to be supernatural. She wouldn't need to manufacture excuses to help Harriet if Harriet was a Charmed Innocent.

"Are you sure you don't want dessert?" Nathaniel asked. "I'm not independently wealthy, but I can afford a dish of ice cream."

"No, I really am full," Paige said. In deference to his grad-student status and handyman's bank account, she had skipped having an appetizer and ordered the stuffed chicken breast special. "I'll just have more coffee."

Paige had thoroughly enjoyed having dinner with the handsome academic. Nathaniel was so positive that magic had no basis in reality, she didn't have to worry about exposing herself as a witch. Not that she would. But there was a certain challenge to the fact that he wouldn't believe her anyway.

During the meal Paige had told Nathaniel about her adventure at Mystic Knoll. He handled the snake incident with the same detached acceptance that Tammy had, except that Nathaniel was sold on electromagnetism being the cause.

Nathaniel leaned back as the waitress set a dish of French vanilla ice cream with a fresh strawberry topping in front of him. "I hope you don't mind if I indulge."

"I don't mind." Paige set her cup down for the waitress to refill.

Nathaniel picked up the conversation where they had left off. "Eventually someone will analyze the physical properties and conditions on the site and figure out why Mystic Knoll has such a powerful influence on things around here."

Paige waited until the waitress left before challenging Nathaniel's premise. "How do you explain the coffee boiling away in cups at the Parfait Café today?"

"It was hot?" Nathaniel grinned.

Paige smiled. She was glad to see a crack in the studious veneer Nathaniel had maintained during dinner. He was serious about finding out why rational, intelligent people were so willing to accept illogical fantasies as fact. He just didn't know he was basing his thesis on a flawed premise.

Paige could have shot multiple holes in Nathaniel's assumptions, but he flatly refused to address the concept of real magic, even as a what-if. Over coffee and dessert she couldn't resist needling him, to inject some fun into the discussion.

"It's possible the elemental makeup and configuration of the stones may have something to do with the variety of effects and objects affected," Nathaniel said.

"The tour guide's patter mentions a curse," Paige said.

"Yes, I've been here long enough to have heard most of the stories in town." Nathaniel shook his head, then shrugged. "Urban legends are a powerful force."

"Apparently," Paige said. She had promised to find out what she could about Ida and Harriet for Phoebe, but she didn't want Nathaniel to question her interest. Busybodies didn't usually mean well.

"Piper and Leo heard that Harriet's mother—" Paige faltered, drawing a blank on the name.

"Abigail," Nathaniel said.

"Right. Thanks." Paige took a sip of coffee and went on. "A shopkeeper said Abigail 'bewitched' her father into hanging himself, and my tour guide thinks Abigail hexed the town."

"Unfortunately the Thornwoods have a colorful personal history that invites speculation." Nathaniel swallowed a spoonful of ice cream, then picked up his coffee cup.

Paige had the feeling he was weighing what and how much he should say next. Curbing her curiosity, she waited.

"I guess it can't hurt to tell you," Nathaniel said finally. "I felt guilty—but relieved—after I talked to your sister this afternoon."

"Why is that?" Paige asked.

"Guilty for discussing people I care about

behind their backs," Nathaniel explained. "And relieved because I may be the only person in this town who *does* care about them, and Phoebe's obviously worried about Harriet too."

"She is." Paige picked up her coffee spoon and snitched a bite of Nathaniel's ice cream. "We all are—and we want to help, if there's any way we can."

"Well, it's a long, sad story." Nathaniel pushed the ice-cream dish toward Paige and rested his arms on the table. "You've probably noticed that the people in this town like to talk."

"I noticed," Paige said, smiling warmly.

Nodding, Nathaniel began his tale. "Ida was the oldest of seven girls, twenty-six, and a spinster when her father arranged her marriage with Joshua—to get her off the farm."

Paige sighed. "I take it Ida would have preferred spinsterhood."

"And no one could blame her if she did," Nathaniel said. "Joshua was a cruel man. Ten years older than Ida, and he had a violent temper. The only reason he wanted a wife was so he wouldn't have to pay hired help at the Yankee Bear."

Paige frowned but didn't interrupt.

"Ida took care of everything," Nathaniel continued. "She cooked, cleaned, kept the books, did the laundry. They say she hardly ever left the property, and unless she was abnormally accident-prone, Joshua beat her too."

Paige clenched her jaw. Unspoken in Nathaniel's narrative was the fact that the town knew about the abuse and did nothing to help. She made a mental note to tell Phoebe. Abused people often grew up to become abusers.

"I can't imagine going through life like that," Paige said, prompting Nathaniel to go on.

Nathaniel nodded. "That's why Ida wanted a baby. She thought a child would bring some joy into her drab existence. Except Abigail was born just as calculating and cruel as her father."

"Nobody is born calculating," Paige said. *However*, she finished in her mind, *some people are born evil*. She wanted to see if Nathaniel brought up the other rumors floating around Cairn about Abigail. An *ordinary* teenager couldn't get revenge by blackening teeth and making hair fall out.

"Maybe not," Nathaniel agreed. "But Abigail couldn't catch a break—from the moment she entered this world to the moment she left it. She had a disfiguring birthmark that set her up for relentless peer ridicule and a father who refused to acknowledge or speak to her."

"No wonder she was mad at the world," Paige said.

"Furious, which is why everyone was so quick to believe she killed Joshua," Nathaniel explained. "And nobody was upset when she died two years later."

"Leaving Ida with the responsibility of raising Harriet," Paige said. She knew from Phoebe that Ida had inherited the Yankee Bear from her husband and couldn't leave her only source of income.

"And she's never complained," Nathaniel said. "Not a word."

"But Harriet's practically a prisoner at the inn," Paige countered. "Just like Ida was with Joshua."

"Harriet has fits," Nathaniel said, rising to Ida's defense, "and Ida's protecting her. She closes the inn three days a month because Harriet's episodes are worse the three days of the new moon."

"The new moon is this weekend?" Paige didn't keep track of the lunar phases unless she needed to know them for a spell.

"Sunday." Nathaniel motioned for the waitress to bring the check. Then he glanced back at Paige. "Are you sure you don't want anything else?"

"No, I'm fine." Paige smiled, thinking that it had been much too long since she had enjoyed a dinner date.

"Are you ready?" Nathaniel asked. He tucked cash into a leather folder with the check and pushed it aside. He'd left a generous tip.

"Yes." Paige nodded. "This was very nice, thank you."

Nathaniel was quiet on the ride back to the Yankee Bear, giving Paige time to mentally sort through all he had said. She still had questions, but she couldn't ask the nonbelieving grad student about anything related to magic.

However, she was almost certain that the detour to Mystic Knoll in Cairn, New Hampshire, had not been an accident. Their New England vacation, if they ever got to finish it, was a perk of being on a Charmed assignment.

"We're here," Nathaniel said, breaking into Paige's thoughts. He shifted the truck into neutral and pulled on the emergency brake. Then he jumped out to open her door and walked her to the porch.

Paige was sorry to have the evening end so soon. She wasn't in the market for a serious romance, but she wouldn't refuse a kiss. Although he was inflexible and totally wrong-headed about magic, Nathaniel was a nice guy.

"I really did enjoy myself tonight, Nathaniel."

"So did I." Nathaniel clasped Paige's hand for a second, then released it. "See you tomorrow."

Paige stared as Nathaniel dashed back to his truck. He obviously couldn't wait to get away.

What, she wondered, *did I say or do to turn him off?*

Chapter

6

"Does it always take Leo this long to shave, Piper?" Phoebe asked. She sat in a wingback chair by the window in Piper and Leo's room, tapping her foot impatiently.

"Are we in a rush?" Piper pulled blue denim bib shorts and a white T-shirt out of Wyatt's suitcase. "When do we have to leave?"

"Two o'clock and not a minute later," Phoebe said, mimicking the old woman's gravelly voice. "Roughly."

"That doesn't give us much time." Paige perched on the bed across from Piper.

"Time for what?" Piper picked up Wyatt off a blanket on the floor and sat him next to her on the bed.

"To find out what's up with this town," Paige said. "Like why everything seems to go bonkers."

"Is Mystic Knoll magical or just a really weird scientific anomaly?" Phoebe added, leaning forward. She rested her arms on her knees. "And what's the connection to Harriet?"

Paige continued the list of questions that needed answers: "And was Abigail a witch? Tammy thinks she cast spells to make bad things happen."

"Maybe she was just a gifted practitioner," Phoebe offered.

"Okay, okay, I get your point . . . s," Piper said, holding up a hand to stop them. She was aware that she was being obstinate. It wasn't that she didn't want to help if Charmed intervention was needed. She just wasn't ready to completely abandon her vacation for a magical wild-goose chase.

"Harriet needs our help." Phoebe's tone implied that should be obvious.

Piper resisted the urge to point out that Harriet's problems were tragic but not necessarily the result of supernatural evil.

Paige stood up and started to pace. "And Mystic Knoll is just too intriguing to ignore."

Piper looked at the determined expressions on her sisters' faces and decided not to argue. When they were like this, she knew she wouldn't win; besides, there was always the possibility that her sisters were right. "Okay," she said, sighing. "So what's your plan?"

Phoebe didn't hesitate. "I'm going into town to

find out about Harriet's father. Nobody has said anything about him. We don't know who—or maybe even *what*—he was."

"What about you, Paige?" Piper pulled on Wyatt's shorts and fastened the straps.

"I'll stay here," Paige said. "Nathaniel said Harriet's fits get worse around the new moon, which just happens to be tomorrow. Besides, he might know more than he told me last night."

Wyatt giggled, rolled over, and started to crawl away.

"So your date went well?" Piper grabbed Wyatt's ankle and glanced at Paige.

"Right up until he left me with a handshake." Paige's eyes narrowed, warning against a follow-up question. "What are you and Leo up to?"

"We're going to the used bookstore." Piper wrangled the playful Wyatt onto his back and reached for his shoes and socks.

"What's he looking for?" Paige asked.

"Books." Piper didn't specify that Leo was trying to replace his collection of paperbacks she had accidentally blown up while cleaning the closet. "No promises, but I'll nose around a little too."

Leo sauntered through the door and tossed his shaving kit on the bed. "Bathroom's free."

Phoebe glanced at Paige. "Do you mind if I go first? I need to ride into town with Piper and Leo."

"No. But there are two bathrooms," Paige reminded her.

"Yeah, but the shower in the other one spits."

Phoebe flicked her fingers open and closed to illustrate a spastic water spray.

"Don't take forever," Leo said as Phoebe walked by.

"That's okay. We're not quite ready." Piper held up a small shoe. "No bye-bye until the shoes are on the feet, Wyatt. Uncurl those toes."

Wyatt stuck his feet in the air and pulled off his socks.

Fifteen minutes later Piper, Leo, and Phoebe took their complimentary coffee and doughnuts to go and packed Wyatt into the van. Due to heavy Saturday traffic on the two-lane highway, the drive into Cairn took longer than it had the day before. Several cars ahead of them slowed to turn into Mystic Knoll, but a sign had been posted that the site was temporarily closed.

After they dropped Phoebe off at city hall, they had to circle the public parking lot, waiting for a parking space to open up. Piper couldn't dispel a surge of anxiety as Leo flipped open the stroller and set Wyatt inside. She was wary and vigilant on the three-block walk, but her apprehension was unnecessary. Birds did not explode out of the trees, and ants did not swarm through cracks in the sidewalks. She hadn't realized she was waiting for something to happen until they pushed the stroller into the bookstore.

"Morning." A gray-haired man with a pleasant face sat behind a wooden counter piled high with books.

"Hi," Piper said with a quick glance around.

Almost every available space in the store was piled with books. They were stacked on the shelves behind the clerk and on the floor around him. Public notices, yard-sale flyers, and business cards were tacked to a bulletin board on the wall. Next to it a faded picture of a rainbow trout marked the month of June on a 1976 calendar.

On the customer side of the counter, floor-to-ceiling bookcases covered the walls and formed aisles down the length of the narrow room. Every shelf was jammed with leather-bound and paper volumes. Stacks of children's books, magazines, and romance novels covered a table and three mismatched chairs. Two smaller bookcases were filled with old science-fiction and fantasy magazines and pulp paperbacks.

A forty-gallon freshwater aquarium stood in front of the window display. The lower shelf on the black metal tank stand was devoted to books about tropical fish.

"Brad York," the man said, half rising and extending his hand. "You folks looking for anything in particular?"

"Actually, I have a list." Leo shook Brad's hand, then pulled a worn paper from his wallet. He had made the list immediately after Piper confessed that she had turned his favorite novels into confetti. He crossed off the titles as he replaced them.

"Let's see it." Brad took the paper and put on

wire-rimmed glasses to read it. "I think we have a few of these. I'll just need a minute or two to find them."

"A minute or two?" Leo's gaze darted across the store's chaotic shelves. "You know where everything is in here?"

"Yep." Smiling, Brad nodded and pulled a laptop out from under the counter. "I just have to check my database."

Leo sagged with a sheepish grin. "I'll just look around while you're doing that."

"I'll wait here with Wyatt," Piper said. "It's too crowded in here for little hands that like to touch."

"Let's see what we can do about that." Brad reached under the counter again. "Have a green—"

As Brad raised his arm, Piper froze him.

Leo looked up from the old magazine he was leafing through. "What are you doing?"

"Protecting Wyatt." Piper pointed to the seven-inch-long piece of round, green plastic with embedded glitter dangling from Brad's fingers. "What is that?"

Leo stepped up to look. "A fake worm for fishing."

"Oh." Piper smiled tightly, then joked to break the tension. "Places, everyone!" As soon as Leo was back in position, she unfroze the scene.

"—sparkly." Brad placed the plastic worm in Wyatt's eager hand.

"Guh!" Wyatt closed his fingers around the green sparkly and shook it vigorously.

"Have a seat, Mom." Brad waved at the chairs. "Just dump that stuff on the floor."

"Okay." Piper lifted the stack of magazines and set them on the floor. She positioned Wyatt's stroller so he could see the fish tank, then sat down.

"You folks here to watch the solar eclipse tomorrow?" Brad asked. He squinted at the laptop, then typed in a title.

"No, we just stopped overnight on our way south," Piper said.

"I'm surprised you found a room." Brad jotted a note in a small, spiral-bound memo pad. "Cairn doesn't have many motels, and they fill up quick when something special's going on."

"Really?" Piper tried to sound surprised. "We're the only guests at the Yankee Bear."

Brad looked up sharply. He *was* surprised. "Ida kept the Yankee Bear open last night?"

"Is that unusual?" Piper asked, frowning with fake puzzlement.

"Yep." Brad looked back at the computer screen. "She's been closing three days out of every twenty-eight without fail for years. Don't know why."

Piper waited for Brad to continue, but he started typing on the laptop instead. Maybe he didn't know that Ida closed because Harriet's fits were worse during the new moon. Or, unlike the other people she had met in Cairn, he just didn't want to talk about the neighbors.

"Running that inn must be a lot of work, even with a handyman," Piper said. "Ida probably just wants a few days off every month."

"Maybe." Brad made another note on the pad. "She never got time off when Joshua was alive. That's for sure. Twenty-two years of love-less drudgery and a hellion child to boot."

"Yeah," Piper said. "We heard that Abigail was difficult."

"Well, you heard right." Brad shook his head. "Abigail was doomed from the get-go."

"Why?" Piper hoped Brad wouldn't balk at her curiosity. So far he hadn't told her anything she didn't already know. But she had the feeling he knew more than he was telling.

"Some folks just can't help being supersti-tious," Brad said. "They think Mystic Knoll has supernatural power and that Abigail's birth-mark was a brand. Her own father thought evil had an irrevocable claim on her soul. If you ask me, Joshua's rejection and the town's ridicule drove the good right out of that girl."

"I guess being an outcast could poison a per-son's life," Piper agreed, "but it's hard to believe Abigail did everything the people around here think she did."

"Like making Ned Johnson's cat's toe wither and fall off because it scratched her?" Brad arched an eyebrow. "Wasn't witchcraft. Spider bite."

"Can spiders do that?" Piper asked.

"Doc Randall thinks so." Brad closed the laptop. "If I thought Abigail was a witch, then I'd have to believe she tried to drown my daughter."

"What happened?" Piper asked.

"Molly pushed Abigail into a pool at a kid's birthday party." The man sighed, shaking his head. "The next weekend Molly almost drowned in Saunders Pond. She said she forgot how to swim. I think she just panicked, but she never went into the water again."

"That's sad," Piper said.

"Yes, but it wasn't magic." Brad seemed determined to put the rumors about Abigail Thornwood to rest, at least in her mind. "Abigail was proud, cruel, and defiant, but she couldn't cast spells. That's just an easy out for everyone who tormented her."

"Still, casting spells is an odd thing for people to assume," Piper prodded.

"They assumed it because that's what Abigail wanted them to assume," Brad explained.

Piper was inclined to agree with part of that assessment. Dabbling in witchcraft often gave troubled teenage girls a false sense of empowerment over pressures and forces they couldn't control. The majority of them outgrew the need for imagined abilities.

Practitioners had an affinity for magic that allowed them to tap into and use *external* sources of power. Only a few ever discovered actual talent. Witches possessed a magical essence, an *internal* spring from which their power flowed.

Was Abigail a practitioner or a witch? Piper suspected Ida's daughter had been a practitioner, perhaps with a convenient source of power at Mystic Knoll.

"Raising Abigail must have been hard on her mother," Piper said. She felt a sudden sympathetic kinship with Ida. Wyatt wasn't evil, but humanity might perceive him as a threat, and evil coveted his powers.

"Joshua and Abigail hardened Ida's heart, but they couldn't break her," Brad said.

The fake worm went flying out of Wyatt's hand. He started to scream.

"Sorry." Piper quickly retrieved the plastic lure. Wyatt stopped crying the instant she gave it back. "Looks like I'll have to buy the worm, too."

"I don't know if I can sell *that* worm." Brad held his hands eighteen inches apart. "I once caught a bass this big with that sparkly."

"How big?" Piper blinked.

"Big enough," Brad said, grinning. "I threw him back. That fish had lived too long to end up in my frying pan."

"That fish fell for a fake worm," Piper joked. She couldn't tell if Brad was serious.

"Fish don't know the worm is plastic until it's too late." Brad chuckled. "And since you let me tell that fish story, Wyatt can keep the worm. No charge."

Leo wandered back carrying two books. "How did you make out with the list?"

"Found three." Brad lifted his memo pad. "Now, this one by F. Scott Fitzgerald is a first edition—"

Brad stopped talking when a black angelfish landed on the lid of his closed laptop.

Wyatt squealed.

Piper spun toward her son. All the fish in the aquarium began jumping out, but it was too late to freeze the scene. Brad had already seen the flying fins.

"I hate to ask this . . ." Brad pulled two fish-nets out of a jar holding pencils, pens, and scissors on the counter. He handed one to Leo and carefully slid the black angelfish into the other. "Get that swordtail by your foot, will you?"

"Has this happened before?" Leo stooped and flipped the yellow fish into the net with his finger.

"Last time I lost three because I couldn't get to them before they died." Brad hustled back to the tank with the angelfish. "It's been a long time since I remember having so many startling incidents so close together, though."

Bugs, toads, birds, snakes, and now fish, Piper thought.

As Leo stood up he caught a vibrant blue fish in the net before it hit the floor.

Brad dumped the angelfish into the tank. He took a third net off a hook on the stand and gave it to Piper. "You needed a fish story to tell, right?"

Wyatt shook his plastic worm and laughed.

I'm glad someone's having a good time, Piper thought. Checking to make sure Brad's back was turned, she froze an ugly, flopping bottom-feeder before she picked it up.

Phoebe cupped her hand around her face to peer through the window of the *Cairn Clarion* office. The old newspaper building stood across the street from a textile plant that had been converted into office space. Both buildings sported window boxes filled with purple, pink, and white petunias.

Leo and Piper had dropped her off at city hall to check the public records for Harriet Thornwood's father, but the government offices were closed for the weekend. Then she realized the best source of information in any town was the local newspaper.

"Come on in," a woman said. "The door's open."

Phoebe straightened and turned toward the red-headed woman smiling from the doorway. Dressed in jeans and a sweatshirt, she had perfect teeth and wore no makeup to soften an angular, freckled face. She looked thirty-five, but could be a fit-and-trim fifty.

"It's Saturday," Phoebe said. "I wasn't sure—"

"We only publish three days a week, but

Saturday is one of them." The woman stepped back and held the door open for Phoebe. "You can place an ad, but it won't come out until Tuesday."

"Actually, I'm doing some research," Phoebe said. She pulled out her *Bay Mirror* press pass as she stepped inside.

The woman studied Phoebe's credentials, then nodded. "San Francisco. You're a long way from home, Ms. Halliwell."

"Just call me Phoebe."

"Florence Nestor-Haynes." Florence closed the door. "Editor, publisher, reporter, and sometimes I run the presses."

"I've never even *seen* our presses," Phoebe said.

"If I hadn't learned every aspect of the business, my father would have closed the *Clarion* rather than let me have it when he died." A sparkle brightened Florence's brown eyes. "I objected strenuously, but he was right."

"So you're carrying on the family tradition." Phoebe followed Florence through a waist-high swinging door in the front counter.

"Yes, and hoping my son will carry on after me." Florence sat down at a large wooden desk and pointed Phoebe to an empty chair. "Right now, Troy would rather play basketball and video games."

"He must be a teenager," Phoebe said, sitting down.

"Seventeen," Florence said. "Now, what can I do for you?"

Just because other people in Cairn liked to gossip, Phoebe couldn't assume the newspaper editor was a talker too. She had a cover story ready.

"I enjoy working at the *Bay Mirror*, but eventually I want to write a book," Phoebe said. She *was* putting a book proposal together.

"You and a thousand other reporters," Florence said.

Phoebe let the subtle put-down slide. If Florence thought she was just another reporter chasing literary glory, the editor might be more cooperative.

"I like to read thrillers," Phoebe said, "and poke around newspaper archives looking for material I might be able to use someday."

"How long have you been here?" Florence asked.

"Two days," Phoebe said. Her intuition kicked in when she met the other woman's steady gaze. Florence Nestor-Haynes was no fool. If Phoebe wanted the editor's help, she had to be honest. "Long enough to hear some intriguing rumors."

"I bet." Florence laughed. "Well, I've been a journalist long enough to know you'll dig until you find out what you want to know. So you might as well get the facts."

"That's why I came to the *Clarion*," Phoebe said. "To get the facts."

"We've got everything on microfiche in the

back. Everyone in town reads the *Clarion*," Florence explained. "I don't have an online edition—yet."

Phoebe followed Florence through the large back area that housed the presses, to a small room filled with supplies and boxes of old copies of the newspaper. The microfiche equipment sat on a long table in the corner. Phoebe sat on a folding chair in front of the reader.

"Let me know if you need anything else," Florence said. She closed the door when she left.

Phoebe had so many questions about Abigail Thornwood she wasn't sure where to start. She went back twenty-two years and searched for articles about Joshua Thornwood's death. The story had made the front page and was written by Frank Nestor. Phoebe assumed Frank was Florence's father. The headline read: SUICIDE OR MURDER?

According to the article, the sheriff found Joshua Thornwood's body hanging from a rafter in the attic of the Yankee Bear. The day before, three people had heard Abigail tell him he should do everyone a favor and break his neck.

"That's creepy," Phoebe mumbled, shuddering. The more she learned about Abigail, the more certain she was that Ida's daughter had been a sociopath. Abigail had known right from wrong, but had never suffered a moment's remorse for any harm she had done.

Abigail may have inherited the personality disorder from her father, Phoebe realized suddenly.

Considering the stories Paige and Piper had heard, Joshua had also exhibited traits common to an antisocial personality. Ironically, Ida had wanted a baby to *relieve* the misery Joshua caused her. Instead the child had just brought her more grief.

Phoebe read the rest of the article. Oddly, Abigail had not been arrested. She had been sitting in the town square when Joshua drove back to the inn that night. She was still sitting there when Ida called the sheriff to report her husband's death four hours later. Five witnesses swore Abigail hadn't left the park.

The article ended with the question, did Abigail kill her father with the power of suggestion?

Creepier and creepier, Phoebe thought. Apparently Mabel and Angus at the antique shop weren't the only ones who thought it was possible Abigail had "bewitched" her father. Frank Nestor had not dismissed the possibility either.

Next Phoebe looked up births for twenty years ago. Harriet's arrival and Abigail's death of natural causes were combined in a short column. Abigail had been survived only by her newborn daughter and her mother. There was no reference to the baby's father.

"But somebody's responsible," Phoebe muttered. On a hunch she searched the society pages for the previous year. "Bingo."

There was a reference to Abigail in a weekly

gossip column called "High Times." Abigail had gone to the senior prom with Lucas Barnes—nine months before Harriet was born. The author of the article, Linda Cambridge, wondered, "Why did Lucas Barnes, star quarterback and best looking guy in the senior class, ask Abigail Thornwood to be his date? Is it possible Abigail really can cast spells? Nothing else explains this social mismatch!"

Phoebe wondered too. Had Abigail used a spell to get a date for the prom—and a baby? Since Lucas wasn't mentioned in Harriet's birth announcement, he hadn't admitted to being her father. *What did Abigail do to get revenge on him?*

Phoebe found several references to Lucas Barnes in the years since Harriet was born. He had graduated from the University of New Hampshire, returned to Cairn to teach at the high school, married, and had a son of his own. Lucas had escaped Abigail's wrath.

Perhaps, Phoebe mused, Abigail had hoped Lucas would change his mind about meeting his responsibilities after the baby was born. Instead Abigail had died in childbirth, and Lucas was off the hook. He had abandoned Abigail and his daughter both.

With her fact-finding mission completed, Phoebe turned the machine off. On her way out of the building, she stopped to thank Florence for her help.

"Glad to do it," Florence said, smiling with

genuine warmth. "Was your search a success?"

"Very much so," Phoebe said. "I read a couple of your dad's articles about Abigail Thornwood."

"Abigail wasn't one of his favorite people," Florence said. "When she was twelve, my dad yelled at her for running through his flowerbeds."

"What happened?" Phoebe asked.

"All the flowers died," Florence said.

Very creepy, Phoebe thought. She thanked Florence again and left.

Back outside, Phoebe tried to untangle her conflicted impressions. She didn't blame Lucas for rejecting Abigail, especially if the girl had used magic to seduce him. But Abigail was dead, and that made it harder to forgive him for turning his back on Harriet.

Phoebe started walking and pulled out her cell phone. Unless they heard from her, Leo and Piper would return to city hall to pick her up in an hour. She dialed Piper's cell to say she had finished early, but she couldn't get a signal.

The first pay phone Phoebe found was outside Stark's Pharmacy. A phone book was attached to the stand with a heavy, coiled wire. She turned to the yellow pages to look up the used bookstore, then flipped back to the residence section. There was one listing for Lucas Barnes. She wrote the address and phone number down and went into the drugstore.

"Excuse me," Phoebe asked a teenage girl at

the front counter. The name "Nancy" was embroidered on the girl's polo shirt. "I need directions to Prospect Street."

"It's about ten blocks that way." The girl pointed out the door. "Turn left on Cove by city hall. Prospect is the street before the high school."

A few blocks farther on, Phoebe tried her cell phone again, but Cairn was apparently out of signal range for her provider. If Piper and Leo got to city hall before she did, they'd just have to wait.

The distance between side streets in Cairn varied, and most of the stretches were shorter than the average city block in San Francisco. Prospect intersected Cove at the four-hundred block. She turned right and walked two and a half more blocks to number 629. The names Lucas, Anne, and Tim Barnes were printed on the mailbox.

Phoebe gritted her teeth as she turned up the front walk. Apparently Lucas had a pleasant family life—one he wasn't willing to share with Harriet.

Flowers grew on both sides of the flagstone path leading up to a modest Cape Cod house. A basketball hoop was attached to the one-car garage, and a green awning hung over the front door. The porch was too small for furniture, but a plant stand with a large ivy stood in one corner.

Phoebe rang the bell and stepped back. She

wasn't sure what she hoped to accomplish or
even what she wanted to say.

A tall man with broad shoulders, solemn gray
eyes, and dark hair peppered with gray
answered the door. "Yes?"

"I'm sorry to bother you, Mr. Barnes, but"—
Phoebe hesitated, then decided to confront the
issue head-on—"I'd like to talk to you about
Abigail Thornwood."

Fear flashed across the man's tanned face.
Without a word Lucas slammed the door.

Phoebe knocked, but Lucas Barnes didn't
answer. He had locked her out of his house as
definitively as he had locked Harriet out of his life.

Paige sat on the front porch of the Yankee Bear,
watching Nathaniel spread fertilizer on the
lawn. She had been watching him for forty-five
minutes. She had waved, but he hadn't waved
back or even looked in her direction.

At first she thought Nathaniel was concen-
trating on his work and hadn't noticed her. But
as he headed to the garden shed in back, she
knew that he was avoiding her.

If he doesn't want to talk to me, fine, Paige thought.
She stood up and stomped down the steps. *But he's
not going to get off without telling me why.*

Paige caught up with Nathaniel as he opened
the double doors on the large shed. She was
blunt. "Is there a reason you're not speaking to
me today?"

"Hello, Paige." Nathaniel stepped into the shed without meeting her gaze. He lifted the spreader inside and parked it against the back wall.

Paige took a deep breath. Losing her temper would only give Nathaniel a good excuse to ignore her.

"Did Ida ask you not to hang out with the guests?" Paige asked evenly.

"That's not it." Nathaniel wiped his face with a paper towel, then tossed it into a large trash container.

"Then what is it?" Paige knew she sounded annoyed, but she couldn't help it. Something had happened between dessert at the Fish, Fowl, and Cow and the front door of the Yankee Bear last night. She just didn't have a clue what. "No long-distance relationships?"

Nathaniel stepped back to stand in the doorway. "You're very pretty, Paige, and great company. And too intelligent to believe in the paranormal. Or you should be."

Paige just stared at him. It took all her willpower not to orb one of the garden tools into her hand, just to show him he wasn't as smart as he thought he was. *That would take the superior expression off his face in a hurry,* she thought. Unfortunately the Charmed rules didn't make exceptions for converting attractive but insufferable nonbelievers.

"You arrived at this conclusion based on our conversation last night?" Paige asked, puzzled.

"Not until we were driving back here." Nathaniel leaned against the doorjamb. "That's when I realized you thought magic explained the Mystic Knoll anomaly. Only fools believe in curses and hexes."

Paige bit her tongue. She wanted to tell Nathaniel she was a witch and he was the fool, but she couldn't. She couldn't let the insult pass, either.

Paige leaned toward Nathaniel. Her gaze and voice hardened with controlled wrath. "I'd rather believe that magic *might* be real than confine myself to the absolute and totally *boring* certainty that it's not."

"You think I'm boring?" Nathaniel looked stricken.

Paige realized she had struck a nerve, but she had no sympathy. She got in his face to drive her point home.

"You won't be able to finish your thesis, Nathaniel," Paige said, "because you're too narrow-minded to *accept* why rational people cling to illogical belief in the fantastic."

Nathaniel frowned, but he didn't turn away.

"Believing in impossible things keeps people connected to innocence and hope. Didn't you believe in Santa Claus?" Paige asked. "What happened to your sense of wonder?"

"I grew up," Nathaniel said.

"Yeah. Too bad." Paige shrugged, then turned and walked away.

Chapter

7

Phoebe paced from one end of Leo and Piper's room to the other. Finding Harriet's human father had cemented rather than diffused her resolve.

Lucas Barnes had slammed his door in her face. Why? Had Abigail so intimidated him in life he was still afraid twenty years after her death? Was he ashamed for fathering Harriet? Or for forsaking her?

"How can we *not* help Harriet?" Phoebe turned to challenge her sisters and Leo.

"Help her what?" Piper folded Wyatt's pajamas and placed them in his canvas suitcase.

"Escape her tyrant grandmother might be a good place to start." Paige sat on the floor helping Wyatt stuff blocks through the holes in a shape-sorter cube.

"Where would she go?" Piper asked. "What

would she do? I'm not being insensitive. Harriet is barely functional in everyday social situations."

"With good reason," Leo said. He had found one of the socks he had worn yesterday. He bent over to look under the chest of drawers for the other one.

"The fits are a problem," Phoebe admitted as she sat in the wingback chair. According to Nathaniel, Ida had taken Harriet out of school to protect her from the taunts of insensitive classmates. If other residents of Cairn treated Harriet as cruelly as Jed Dalton had the day before, the young woman's reclusive lifestyle was understandable.

"Especially since Harriet's condition may be connected to Mystic Knoll," Leo said. He stuffed a dirty shirt into his duffle.

"Which may or may not be magical." Paige handed Wyatt a square block and grinned when he poked it through the correct hole. "Yea, Wyatt!"

"That's what bothers me." Piper pushed Wyatt's suitcase aside and sat down on the bed.

"What?" Leo asked. He pulled the missing sock out from under the pillow and put it in his bag.

"We don't *know* if Harriet's problem is magical," Piper said. "Or if Mystic Knoll is either. And as much as I'd like to just be on vacation, I can't believe we took a wrong turn and stumbled into this weird town for no reason."

"So you think we were brought here on purpose too," Phoebe said. "To help Harriet."

"Maybe," Piper said, "but that brings us right back to my original question. Help her do what?"

Paige looked up. "Cure her condition?"

"Is it magical or medical?" Piper asked.

"Nathaniel said nothing physical has ever turned up on her tests," Phoebe answered.

"I could orb home to check the Book of Shadows for a reference to Mystic Knoll." Paige opened the plastic cube and dumped the blocks so Wyatt could start over.

"And the Elders might know something," Leo said.

"Then what are you waiting for? The sooner we find out, the sooner we can get on with our vacation—or not." Piper shooed Paige and Leo away with her hands. "Go!"

"Buh!" Wyatt waved bye-bye as his aunt and father dissolved into streams of sparkling light.

Piper lifted Leo's bag onto the bed and pointed to Phoebe. "You play. I'll pack."

"Okay." Phoebe sat on the floor and reached for the block Wyatt had put in his mouth. "It's not nice to eat your toys."

Twenty minutes later Wyatt had fallen asleep in Phoebe's lap. Piper had finished packing—in case they decided or were forced to leave—and was resting on the bed with her arm over her eyes. Phoebe felt a little drained herself. Usually they didn't have to work so hard to determine if their Charmed powers were needed.

Easing Wyatt off her lap so that he was sitting on the floor, Phoebe stood up and stretched. She glanced at her watch, wondering why Leo and Paige were taking so long, then flinched when someone knocked on the door.

Piper sat up, instantly awake. "What's that?"

"Door," Phoebe said. "I'll get it."

"I have your bill!" Ida called from the hall.

Piper slipped off the bed, picked up Wyatt, and moved to the wingback chair.

Ida knocked again, more insistently.

"Coming!" Phoebe smiled and opened the door a few inches. "Hi!"

"It's almost two." Ida held out a handwritten bill.

"And we're almost ready," Phoebe said, stalling. This wasn't the time to discuss whether they were checking out immediately or not.

"I'll be outside cleaning windows," Ida said.

"Okay." As Phoebe reached for the bill she saw the glow of an orb in her peripheral vision.

Leo! Or Paige?

"Thanks!" Phoebe snatched the paper from Ida's hand and closed the door.

Paige had been through the Book of Shadows many times since she had first learned about her heritage. However, familiarity with the pages didn't always make it easy to find what she was looking for. Entries were sometimes added as needed by an ancestor, and other times they simply weren't there to find.

"Like now," she muttered. Frustrated, Paige closed the leather-bound tome. It contained no references to Mystic Knoll, Cairn, or an evil spellcaster called Abigail Thornwood.

Paige scanned the cluttered upper floor of the Manor. Her family had lived in the Victorian house since it was rebuilt after the earthquake in 1906. The memories and paraphernalia of generations had collected in the attic, and they didn't dare throw anything away. Most of the discarded belongings were unremarkable. Other items were enchanted, but as far as she knew, the only way to tell which was which was by luck or accident.

"But since the key to Mystic Knoll isn't here, there's no reason for me to be here either."

Paige no longer needed to concentrate to shift into orb drive. Transforming into a stream of sparkling particles and re-forming had become as natural to her as breathing. A wisp of thought triggered the process in San Francisco, and an instant later she returned to solid form at the Yankee Bear in New Hampshire.

Phoebe sagged against the door as Paige materialized in Leo and Piper's room. Both her sisters looked worried.

"Problem?" Paige asked.

"Ida." Phoebe held up a paper. "The bill."

"She's a little too anxious to get rid of us, if you ask me." Piper sat in the corner with Wyatt cradled in her arms. "What did you find out?"

"Nothing," Paige said as Leo orbed in next to Piper's wingback chair. "There wasn't a word about Mystic Knoll or Abigail in the Book of Shadows. So maybe there isn't anything magical or demonic going on."

"But we can't rule it out," Leo said. "The stone configurations at Mystic Knoll focus and amplify magic. A few witches and shamans knew about the site's power as recently as colonial times, but the knowledge was forgotten over the years."

"Except by the Elders," Phoebe said.

"Yes, and they aren't aware of any impending magical disasters." Leo absently brushed Wyatt's hair back.

Paige recognized the pensive frown Leo often displayed prior to adding a significant "but" to his statements of fact. "But—" she prodded.

"But," Leo said, "total solar eclipses mask magical events and activities, and there will be an eclipse here tomorrow."

Piper's frown reflected confusion. "So something awful *might* happen," she said.

"Tomorrow," Leo repeated.

"But that's *all* we know," Phoebe pointed out with a huff of exasperation.

"Actually, we may know more than we realize." Paige paused to collect the stray thoughts she knew connected in some way. They just hadn't figured out how yet. "Think about it."

"Okay." Phoebe dropped the bill on the nightstand and sat on the bed. She stared at the wall. "We don't *know*, but the wildlife and Harriet are probably affected by magical forces that are either generated or amplified by Mystic Knoll."

"I agree, and the effects are getting worse," Paige said. "Tammy told me there haven't been this many weird incidents this close together since she was a kid."

"Brad said basically the same thing," Piper said. "He owns the bookstore."

"Harriet's twenty years old," Phoebe said, rubbing her chin.

"Is that relevant?" Paige asked.

"I don't know that yet, but some basic, old-fashioned research seems in order." Phoebe stood up. "I can use the phone line in the kitchen to get on the Internet. It might help to know Harriet's birth date, though."

"How do we get it without making Ida suspicious?" Paige asked.

"I saw a Bible in the front sitting room," Leo said. "If Ida doesn't use it to record family dates, I'm sure someone in town would be more than happy to tell us."

"That's for sure," Piper muttered.

"I'll check it out," Paige volunteered. "If the Bible is a bust, I can orb into town and back without being missed."

Leo looked at Phoebe. "What if Ida walks in while you're online?"

"I'm just checking my e-mail." Phoebe shrugged with a what's-the-problem look. "Did she say which windows she was cleaning?"

"Watch Wyatt, Leo." Piper handed him the sleeping boy. "I'll go with Phoebe, just in case she needs an emergency freeze."

Paige looked out the window. "Nathaniel's truck isn't in the driveway, but he could come back anytime too."

Her chest constricted with a pang of regret. If she and Nathaniel wanted to pursue a relationship, being separated by a continent wasn't an insurmountable obstacle. But the chasm created by Nathaniel's chauvinism against magic was too wide to bridge. She couldn't overlook his contempt for those who thought that what could be imagined might also be real.

"Nathaniel doesn't give me the heebie-jeebies," Phoebe said as she started for the door.

Paige followed Piper and Phoebe into the hall and kept going when her sisters stopped to get Phoebe's laptop from the other room. Since she didn't know where Ida was, she walked downstairs with an excuse rehearsed and ready. Ida wasn't visible through the foyer window. Still, as a precaution, Paige grabbed a couple of brochures from the rack before she strolled into the front room.

The Bible sat on a table at the far end of a

colonial-style sofa. Several magazines were fanned on the coffee table, an invitation for guests to sit and relax. Although Ida wasn't at the front-room windows either, Paige sat down and flipped through the pamphlets. She heard Piper and Phoebe come down the stairs and turn into the hall. She waited another minute, then opened the Bible.

There were very few entries on the ornamental family pages in the middle of the book. Beginning with Joshua's birth in 1925, Ida had recorded her own birthday, her wedding day, and Abigail's birthday. Her daughter's death had occurred the same day Harriet was born, on May 19, 1985.

Paige committed the date to memory and stuffed the brochures in her pocket. As she rose to leave, the sound of metal hitting wood warned her that Ida was nearby. In danger of being trapped with no options except to be seen, to orb, or to wait, she walked toward the foyer. Something, perhaps a bucket, banged against the house again. She glanced back, but the old woman had not reached the sitting-room windows.

Paige hurried down the hall, opened the kitchen door, and ducked inside.

Phoebe sat hunched over her laptop at the built-in table with attached booths. Sitting across from her, Piper whipped her head around and raised her hands to freeze.

"It's just me!" Paige whispered, closing the door behind her. "How are you doing?"

"We're making progress," Piper said. "Solar eclipses only happen during the new moon."

That makes sense, Paige thought, recalling what she had learned in a college astronomy course.

The moon circled Earth every twenty-eight days. The new phase was dark because the moon passed between Earth and the sun, and sunlight reflected off the side facing away from Earth. During a solar eclipse, the moon passed directly in front of the sun, blocking the light. Whether or not a total or partial eclipse could be seen was determined by the observer's location on Earth.

"And Harriet's episodes are the worst during the new moon," Phoebe added.

"Did you get her birth date?" Piper asked.

"May nineteenth, 1985." Paige stayed by the door so she could hear if anyone approached.

"Bingo," Phoebe said.

"What?" Paige asked.

Phoebe looked up from the computer screen. "The last total eclipse in this area happened in 1985, a month before Harriet was born."

"What's the significance of that?" Paige asked.

"I certainly don't know," Piper said. "It just raises more questions."

"If we want answers, maybe we should go

straight to the source and ask Harriet." Phoebe disconnected from the Internet and shut down her laptop.

"If she'll talk to us." Piper slid out of the booth.

Paige cracked the door and waved her sisters into the empty hall.

"Where's Ida?" Phoebe whispered as they crept toward Harriet's room.

"She was still cleaning windows a few minutes ago." Paige knocked softly on Harriet's door.

"Grandma?" Harriet asked, her voice muffled by the heavy door.

Phoebe stepped up to the door. "It's Phoebe, Harriet. We talked yesterday." When there was no reply, she tried again. "Can I come in?"

"No! No, no, no!" Harriet yelled. Within a second or two, her shouts became increasingly hysterical.

"Try the door," Paige said, her expression worried.

Phoebe turned the knob, but the door was locked. "Ida must have locked her in again."

Harriet shrieked and spewed nonsensical gibberish. Then, judging by the sound of unidentified objects hitting the walls, she began to throw things. Then something repetitively hit the bedroom door.

"Is she banging her head against the door?" Phoebe asked.

"I can orb in to find out," Paige said.

"You've got to orb in to stop her," Piper said, "before she hurts herself."

Phoebe nodded. "I agree."

"Then it's unanimous," Paige said. The Charmed Ones never risked using magic in front of witnesses except in extreme circumstances. This time Harriet's safety outweighed the concerns about revealing Paige's power.

Besides, Paige thought, *Harriet has seen a lot of really weird stuff in this town.* Mystic Knoll may have deadened the shy young woman's capacity for surprise. In addition, she rarely spoke to anyone except her grandmother and Nathaniel. Nathaniel wouldn't believe Harriet had seen a lady made of light, and Ida wouldn't expose her granddaughter to more town ridicule.

A second before Paige began to dissolve, Ida turned the corner into the hall.

"What are you—"

Piper whirled to freeze her.

Not good, Paige thought as she streamed inside Harriet's room. The young woman continued shrieking as she re-formed.

Harriet wore a shapeless nightdress that was stained and torn. Long strands of tangled, dark hair hung in her face. The purple bruise on her arm had changed to greenish yellow.

Paige choked back a rush of pity and desperately tried to calm the young woman. "It's okay, Harriet."

Harriet grabbed her own hair and kept screaming, too terrified to realize the intruder wasn't a
threat.

"Paige!" Phoebe pounded on the door.
"What's happening in there?"

"Oh, nothing," Paige muttered, at a loss for
what to do. She was afraid that shock and sus-
tained fright might cause Harriet unintended
harm. Piper could calm and quiet the young
woman instantly, but Piper's magic hands were
on the other side of the door.

But since Ida was frozen, Paige could orb
Harriet out.

As Paige gripped Harriet's arm, she noticed
two things that destroyed her previous assumptions.

The nails on Harriet's bare feet had thickened, elongated, and curled into hawklike
talons.

And a key was in the lock.

Harriet had locked the door from the inside.

Chapter
8

Piper leaned against the wall and massaged her throbbing temples. She had held out hope that the series of odd, but not totally inexplicable, incidents in Cairn didn't require magical attention. She should have known better. Although the mysterious links among Harriet, Mystic Knoll, and two total solar eclipses twenty years apart weren't conclusive evidence they were knee-deep in a Charmed situation, they now had two witnesses to Paige's traveling light show.

When Harriet's door opened, Piper straightened up and peered inside.

Paige tried to hush the shrieking woman standing just inside the door. She staggered when Harriet suddenly bolted past her into the hall.

"Wait—" Phoebe reached to grab Harriet.

The instant Harriet saw her immobilized

grandmother, she stopped and screamed louder.

"Piper!" Phoebe stuck her fingers in her ears.

Piper froze Harriet. "Okay. Anybody got any more bright ideas?"

"No, but—" Paige pointed downward. "What if Harriet isn't our Innocent?"

Piper stared at Harriet's bare feet. Her toenails had grown into curved, pointed talons. "Did she have those before?"

Phoebe shook her head. "She was barefoot the night we checked in, and I would have noticed the eagle-claw manicure."

"And"—Paige held up a key—"the door was locked from the *inside.*"

Phoebe squinted, puzzled. "Then Ida's the good guy?"

"Let's ask." Before her sisters could object, Piper unfroze the old woman.

"She-devils!" Ida's eyes flashed with revulsion and fear when she saw her granddaughter.

Piper glanced at Harriet. The young woman's face was twisted in a grimace of pure terror. Her expression was a portrait of the pain and panic she had endured throughout her life.

"Monsters!" Ida raised her fists to fight the sisters off as she rushed forward.

"No, we're not." Phoebe grabbed Ida's wrists, stopping her advance.

"Let me go!" Ida snarled and fought to get free.

Not to save herself, Piper realized, but to save

her grandchild. In a moment of crystal clear insight, Piper recognized in the furious old woman the same all-encompassing love that drove Piper to protect Wyatt. No threat was too evil or too dangerous to override that universal maternal instinct.

"Harriet is not hurt!" Phoebe raised her voice, but the meaning of her words didn't pierce Ida's blind rage. Gambling that surprise would break through, Phoebe suddenly released her hold. "We won't hurt you."

Ida stumbled back a step, rubbing her wrists. Her suspicious gaze darted from one to the other before it rested on Harriet. "What did you do to her?"

"Slowed down her molecules," Piper explained.

"She was a little upset," Paige added with an apologetic shrug.

"Can you calm her down if I free her?" Piper asked. When Ida nodded, she unfroze the young woman.

"Grandma!" Harriet burst into tears and threw her arms around the smaller woman.

"It's all right, Harriet." A few inches shorter and thirty pounds lighter, Ida was in danger of suffocating within the terrified girl's crushing embrace. She didn't struggle, but spoke in soothing tones that coaxed Harriet to loosen her hold. "I'm here. It's okay."

The comfort conveyed in those few short

sentences cemented Piper's revised opinion. Ida cherished Harriet and would do anything to keep her safe. *Even yell at her,* Piper thought. She hadn't had to reprimand Wyatt—yet—but she knew she'd be devastated every time she stung him with harsh words for his own good.

Harriet cowered against her grandmother and glanced at the three sisters with frightened brown eyes. Her skin had a raw quality, the result of the peeling Phoebe had seen.

Ida gently pushed Harriet away. "Let's get you back into your room."

Harriet clutched Ida's shirt and wouldn't move until Piper, Paige, and Phoebe eased back. They pretended not to notice her hobbling gait or the click of her deformed nails on the wooden floor. As soon as the two women were through the bedroom door, the three witches quickly followed.

It was the most depressing bedroom Piper had ever seen. The gloom was oppressive; she had to pause inside the door to adjust.

Heavy drapes were drawn over a single window to keep out the day. The glow of a small bed lamp did little to brighten the artificial twilight. Sparse furnishings—a bed, chest of drawers, desk, and chair—added to the dreary ambience. No mirror or picture broke the monotony of faded wallpaper on four walls. Books and clothes were scattered where Harriet had thrown them. There were no knickknacks, jewelry, or photographs,

nothing that hinted of a vibrant personality buried
under Harriet's bleak, defeated demeanor.

"At the risk of being pushy," Phoebe said,
"we have to talk, Ida."

Ida walked Harriet to the bed. "The only
thing we have to talk about is paying your bill so
you can check out."

"No, we have to talk about Mystic Knoll and
Harriet," Piper said. "We're here to help her."

"Nobody can help me," Harriet mumbled.
She crawled into the corner and wrapped her
arms around her knees. "She did it, and someone had to pay."

Abigail? Piper wondered. And why was
Harriet saddled with her mother's debt to society?

"Try to rest." Ida jostled Harriet's shoulder
until the girl stretched out. The old woman
picked up a blanket and noticed that one corner
was shredded. She tossed it aside and pulled
another out from under the bed. After covering
Harriet, she waved Piper and her sisters out.
"We can talk in the kitchen." On their way out,
Piper watched from the corner of her eye as Ida
locked her granddaughter's door.

Phoebe studied the older woman as they filed
into the kitchen. She had accurately defined
some of Ida's character traits, but she didn't
have all the pieces yet. Ida was stubborn, confi-
dent, and stoic. And although her affection for
her afflicted granddaughter seemed genuine,

she might also be the cause of Harriet's damaged psyche.

"Would anyone like tea?" Ida picked up the kettle from the large stove and walked to the sink.

"Yes, please." Paige said. "We all would," she added when Phoebe and Piper nodded.

"Why does Harriet think she's being punished for her mother's actions?" Piper slid into the booth at the built-in table.

"Good question," Paige said, sliding in beside her.

Exactly what I want to know, Phoebe thought, setting her laptop on the counter. She sat in the booth opposite her sisters, keeping an eye on Ida.

"Because she is." Ida turned the gas burner on under the kettle.

"By whom?" Phoebe asked, taken aback by an answer she hadn't anticipated.

"Her mother," Ida said.

Again Phoebe was caught off guard. She had expected Ida to accuse the people in Cairn of persecuting Harriet for Abigail's egregious crimes.

"Abigail couldn't command magic without the stones." Ida turned to look at them. Her gaze was direct, her tone matter-of-fact. "But you can."

"Yes," Piper replied. "We're witches."

"Good witches," Paige added quickly, raising

a cautionary finger. "We're not like Abigail."

The exchange answered a few of their questions, Phoebe realized. Abigail had been a practitioner, as they suspected, and she had used Mystic Knoll to augment her limited power. Ida, apparently, knew everything.

"Did Abigail kill her father?" Piper asked.

"Yes." Ida took four mugs and a tin of teabags from a cupboard. "She did a Svengali on the miserable old coot and told him to break his neck. So he hanged himself."

Phoebe only recognized the reference to the fictional evil hypnotist, Svengali, because she liked old black-and-white horror movies. She thought it was ironic that Joshua, who had dominated Ida for his own malicious purposes, had Svengali traits too.

"My daughter used spells to hurt people who hurt her." Ida set a teabag in each mug, then lifted the kettle and poured boiling water.

"Yes, we know," Paige said.

Ida nodded and carried the mugs to the table. "The town likes to talk."

"More than most." Piper took a mug from Ida and blew on the steaming tea.

"But the folks around here only *think* Abigail used magic. I know she did." Ida set the other mugs down and went to the refrigerator.

Phoebe watched her, amazed. The woman's unemotional delivery was more evidence of a remarkably resilient nature. Subjected to the hardships inflicted by Joshua and Abigail, weaker people would have broken down or lashed out. Somehow Ida had processed the torments in a way that preserved her dignity and ability to love.

"How do you know Abigail used magic?" Paige asked.

Ida didn't answer right away. She set a small pitcher of cream on the table and handed everyone a spoon. Then she pulled a step stool over to the coffee counter and opened the upper cabinet. She returned to the table with a blue book.

"Abigail wrote everything down in her diary." Ida placed the book on the table.

Phoebe glanced at the diary as she moved over to make room in the booth for Ida. The vinyl binding had a locking clasp and a pink flower stamped in one corner. "Everything?" Paige asked.

"If it was important," Ida said. "Abigail found out about Mystic Knoll's magical power at the historical society. I can't imagine why Clara Beady let a twelve-year-old girl rummage around in the colonial archives, but she did."

Phoebe didn't interrupt. As often happened with people who had kept traumas and secrets bottled up for a long time, once Ida started talking, she kept talking.

"Easily fooled about helping with a school project, I guess. Clara was almost eighty back then. She's dead now." Ida left the teabag in her mug and took a sip. "Abigail was wicked at the core before she learned magic. Nobody liked her, but no one was afraid of her."

Paige nodded, and Piper silently stirred sugar and cream into her tea. When Ida paused, both resisted the urge to prod, for fear of shutting the old woman down.

Ida stared over her cup at nothing in particular. "The birthmark made things worse, I'm sure, but Abigail was born with something missing. She didn't understand why people wasted time and energy caring for anyone but themselves, because she couldn't. She couldn't even care about the baby inside her."

Ida's voice cracked. She paused to take a sip of tea.

Phoebe realized that Ida's emotional insulation came apart when Harriet was the topic of discussion.

"Abigail wasn't satisfied just giving her peers warts or bad breath," Ida went on. "She made sure they would all worry for a very long time."

"Worry about what?" Phoebe asked.

"Payback," Ida said. "Abigail told Lucas that he and his friends had to be punished for ruining her life. They wouldn't know when or how, but they would pay."

"Do you know?" Paige leaned forward, her hands clasped around her mug.

"Abigail used the power of Mystic Knoll to curse Harriet a month before she was born," Ida said. "My granddaughter will be the instrument of my daughter's revenge against her old tormentors and their children."

"I'm sorry, but"—Piper looked stricken—"how could anyone hate their own child that much?"

"It wasn't a question of hate. It was all about power and winning," Ida explained. "Abigail didn't feel anything for anyone."

A sociopath with magical ability, Phoebe thought. It was an explosively dangerous combination.

"Now, do you young ladies still think you can help Harriet?" Ida asked.

The old woman's expression was one Phoebe had seen before. Ida wanted to believe, but she didn't dare hope.

"Yes, I think we—" Phoebe reached for the diary. As her fingers touched the vinyl cover she was suddenly ripped from the present into Abigail's past. . . .

In the stone maze at Mystic Knoll, Phoebe watched as Abigail paused outside a tunnel entrance framed in stone. Barefoot in a long, black skirt and a white lace top, she was as small in stature as Ida and pregnant. Thick, dark hair fell in waves past her shoulders. She turned to look up.

Even in her vision-trance state, Phoebe's gaze was drawn to the red blotch that covered Abigail's right eye and cheek. She had been pretty, but no one had ever noticed.

As Abigail disappeared into the stone labyrinth, the sunny day dimmed.

The 1985 eclipse, Phoebe thought as the moon began to move across the face of the sun . . . and the stone walls glowed.

Phoebe remembered the phosphorescent lichen Paige had described. The fox fire relative grew abundantly in the heart of the ancient site. Shadow and patches of yellowish bioillumination had formed an eerie truce between light and dark in the underground cavern. Tendrils of lichen created webs of light in alcoves and depressions. Stalactites and stalagmites glistened, and the musty scent of damp debris was permanently embedded in the rock.

Phoebe shifted her perspective as Abigail emerged from a tunnel. The young practitioner skirted large outcroppings of rock at the perimeter. Obviously familiar and comfortable with the surroundings, Abigail climbed onto a raised slab of flat rock in the center of the chamber and paused to modulate her breathing.

Her gaze flicked to each of three large stalagmites spaced at even intervals. She closed her eyes and began to hum a steady, one-note incantation. Within seconds crackling bolts of red lightning appeared in midair. Thunderous booms filled the cavern as the crimson spikes broke through an invisible barrier. Snapping and sizzling, the bolts zoomed about the cavern in frantic spurts before they were attracted to and absorbed by the three cones.

When the stalagmites began to pulse red, Abigail raised her arms to chant:

> *"Cast from creatures of the night,*
> *Fang and claw, leather and flight.*
> *Two times ten shall pass before*
> *They know my vengeance, hear us roar."*

The enormous power unleashed in the cavern filled Phoebe with awe and a grudging respect for Abigail. No one on the higher planes knew about her horrendous spell because the eclipse had hidden the magic.

A chill wind whipped through the cavern . . . and in Phoebe's mind, a scream rent the quiet.

Phoebe didn't have serial visions often. They were too taxing both to sustain and survive on a regular basis. Suddenly, trapped in the trance, she was vaguely aware of the weakness seeping into her body. She ignored it as she watched a younger, more robust version of Ida Thornwood.

Ida stood at the end of a four-poster bed in a room at the Yankee Bear. Sweat drenched Abigail's face and arms as she gripped the uprights and groaned. Harriet was being born.

And Abigail was dying.

"Breathe, Abigail," Ida implored her struggling daughter. "Deep breaths. It will help."

"No help," Abigail whispered, her voice an agonized rasp. "I'm not done here."

"Abigail—" Ida tensed, then bent over the straining young woman.

Another scream reverberated off the ceiling and ended suddenly—with Abigail's life.

Ida's keening cry filled every space as she picked up the small form that had just come into the world.

Phoebe peered at the baby girl, not sure she could believe what the vision showed her.

Another form was superimposed over the infant. The beast resembled a lizard with bat wings, fangs, and talons.

"Abigail! What did you do?" Ida wailed.

Phoebe knew exactly what Abigail had done. She had condemned the daughter in her womb. One day Harriet would become the monstrosity Abigail had conjured to punish her enemies and their offspring. Striking from the grave was the ultimate exercise of power.

Ida had seen the monster her granddaughter would become. For twenty years she had been protecting Harriet from the taunts of her peers, minimizing how many people witnessed her fits, making sure no one saw the temporary physical changes she developed during the new moon, hoping somehow to save Harriet from the cruel fate her mother had devised.

Before the monstrous image had faded completely, Ida wrapped the newborn in a blanket.

She hugged her granddaughter close as the room dissolved . . . and Harriet limped into the cavern.

Phoebe felt light-headed and nauseous as the vision shifted again. Still, she took in every detail as Harriet stumbled to the raised rock slab.

The young woman's eyes were not liquid brown and human, but yellow and reptilian. Shimmering scales had begun to cover her skin.

Since Harriet's birth Ida had not known when the creature would emerge, only that her grand-daughter's condition was worse during the three days of the new moon.

Phoebe realized that Harriet's fully formed talons were a physical manifestation of an imminent transformation—tomorrow, when the solar eclipse would mask the change.

Red magic crackled in glowing stalagmites as Harriet began to chant her mother's spell.

> *"Cast from creatures of the night,*
> *Fang and claw . . .*

Phoebe's vision blurred. She was . . . wrenched back to reality—in a sudden, sickening second—and then she passed out.

Paige was the first to realize that touching Abigail's diary had triggered a vision for Phoebe. Usually her sister was only "gone" for a few seconds. This time the vision lasted some seconds longer.

"Is she all right?" Ida asked.

"She will be," Piper assured her.

"I don't think so." Paige jumped up when Phoebe started to open her eyes and then slumped over the table.

Ida moved out of the booth. "Can I do anything?"

"We don't know what's wrong." Paige shifted into the cushioned seat beside Phoebe and gently raised her head.

"Leo!" Piper yelled.

"I don't think he can hear—" Ida clamped her mouth closed when Leo orbed into the kitchen with Wyatt.

Leo glanced at Ida, then Piper, his eyes questioning the call.

"Phoebe." Piper held out her hands to take Wyatt.

"She fainted coming out of a vision," Paige said. She gave Leo her seat and slipped back into place beside Piper. They could explain how Ida had gotten into the magical loop later.

As Leo took Phoebe's hand, she opened her eyes. "What happened?" he asked.

"Overload, I think." Phoebe fell back against the seat and took a deep breath. "I'll be all right. Just give me a minute."

"I didn't know men could be witches," Ida said.

"He's not a witch. He's an angel." Paige supplied the stock answer, which was easier than trying to define a Whitelighter.

"I see." Ida looked at Wyatt. "Would he like a cookie?"

"Yes," Piper said, smiling tightly when Leo frowned.

Paige realized her brother-in-law was worried about having to erase Ida's memory, which was doable but inadvisable. Memory dusting wasn't an exact magic, and the subjects often lost more than their unauthorized knowledge of magic. On the other hand, good and evil magical types didn't want word of their existence to get around. Mortals always reacted badly.

"I orbed in front of Ida," Paige confessed.

"Right before I froze her," Piper interjected. "But it's okay. Harriet has hawk feet, but she and Ida aren't evil."

"Unlike Abigail, who practiced magic and wrote it all down in a diary." Paige held up the blue book.

"Which Ida read," Phoebe finished. "Then I touched it and went off on a whirlwind tour of Abigail's wicked ways."

"You've been gone less than an hour," Leo said.

Paige couldn't tell if he was appalled because they had exposed themselves or pleased with their progress. "We work fast," she joked.

"Where's Nathaniel?" Leo asked.

"I sent him home." Ida set down a plate of

chocolate-chip cookies. "It's too close to Harriet's bad time."

Obviously he didn't want to hang around to see me, Paige fumed. She had hoped her morning outburst might have made Nathaniel rethink his inflexible attitudes about myths, magic, and those who believed. *Apparently not.*

Wyatt almost leaped off Piper's lap to reach the plate of cookies. She handed him one.

"I know what's happening to Harriet," Phoebe said. When all eyes turned toward her, she added, "I saw Abigail cast the spell that cursed her."

"Is it hopeless?" Ida dragged the kitchen stool over and sat down.

"Curses can be broken," Phoebe said. She took a swallow of cold tea and described everything she had seen and heard.

Since Paige had taken the Mystic Knoll tour, it was easy to envision Abigail on the flat center stone surrounded by bursts of red lightning.

"The red lightning is free magic," Leo said. "Mystic Knoll probably attracts concentrated fragments. Apparently Abigail had the ability to extract it from the ether. The stone configuration absorbs and amplifies power, so the more free magic she captured, the stronger the spells she could cast."

"Abigail used a lot of magic," Paige said. "Why didn't the Elders detect those spells?"

"It's just not feasible or possible to track every

spell and random magical emission," Leo explained.

"And the total solar eclipse masked the curse," Phoebe said. "Abigail knew there would be another eclipse in twenty years, and she designed the curse to take advantage of it."

Paige was more concerned with the present and the future than with the past. "Well, if we don't figure out a way to *break* it, Harriet will turn into a hideous monster tomorrow."

"A Jersey Devil," Ida said. "That's what Abigail called it in the diary."

"May I?" Paige asked, reaching for the diary. When Ida nodded, she released the unlocked clasp and opened the blue book.

As she flipped through the pages, Paige realized that the diary was a journal and a spell book. Abigail had written everything down in a bold script. A few pages included crude diagrams or pictures.

"The Jersey Devil is a colonial myth from 1735," Leo said. "A woman who was suspected of being a witch was so furious about having a thirteenth child, she swore she'd give birth to a devil."

"What did it look like?" Paige asked.

"As the story goes," Leo said, "it was born normal and almost instantly grew into a beast with bat wings, a horse's head, and a dragon's body."

"Like this?" Paige turned the diary so Leo

and Phoebe could see. The head on the creature Abigail had drawn looked more like a seahorse than a terrestrial equine. Otherwise, Leo's description was accurate.

"That's close to what I saw." Phoebe took a cookie off the plate. When Wyatt reached out, she gave it to him and took another. "What did this thing do?"

"It poisoned rivers and lakes and brought other pestilence and hardships to the Pine Barrens of New Jersey," Leo explained. "There have been unverified sightings of the beast over the past three centuries, usually as a harbinger of shipwrecks and wars."

Paige wondered if Nathaniel was familiar with the Jersey Devil myth. It was the type of local legend that might have inspired his thesis. It had definitely inspired Abigail.

"Harriet will go after Abigail's enemies and their children," Ida said softly. Her lined face showed no emotion, and she spoke with a calm that belied the inner turmoil revealed in her eyes.

"I think it's pretty clear we didn't stop here by accident." Piper took a paper napkin from a holder and wiped cookie crumbs off Wyatt's face.

"No question," Phoebe said. "We're here to help Harriet, Ida."

If we can, Paige thought. She stared at the drawing of the monster in Abigail's book.

Harriet was the innocent pawn of a vindictive, spell-casting mother. But what if they couldn't stop her from changing into the savage bestial weapon of Abigail's vengeance? It was a question none of them had considered.

"I'm really worried about Lucas Barnes," Ida said. "He's a decent man. Abigail bewitched him, too."

"I know." Phoebe smiled. "Someone wrote about it in the *Cairn Clarion*."

Ida's sigh was heavy with guilt. "Lucas and his wife, Anne, are teachers at the high school. Tim is on the football team, a quarterback—just like his father."

For a recluse, Ida knew a lot about Lucas Barnes and his family. Perhaps, Paige realized, because he was Harriet's father, and it wasn't his fault.

"It's not just Harriet—" Ida faltered.

"No, it's not," Paige said.

Piper and Phoebe both looked at her.

Paige finished Ida's thought. "Harriet's potential victims are Innocents too."

Piper swallowed hard, and Phoebe paled as the implication of Paige's observation sank in: If they couldn't prevent Harriet's transformation, they might have to destroy the beast to save Abigail's other intended victims.

Chapter
9

Piper looked up from Abigail's diary when Harriet moaned. She waited, ready to freeze the girl at the hint of unusual activity.

They had set up a rotation to watch Harriet overnight. Piper sat on one of two chairs they had brought into the bedroom. A 1960s lamp-table provided a place to set a soda and enough light to read. The glow from the bed lamp on the chest of drawers lit the corner where Ida lay on a rollaway parked beside Harriet's bed.

Piper tensed as Harriet tried to kick her blanket away. The fabric snagged on her claws. She pulled it off, tearing another hole, then rolled onto her side and fell back into a fitful sleep.

Ida was so exhausted and relieved to have help with her monthly vigil, the disturbance didn't wake her.

"False alarm. Good," Piper mumbled.

The night had not been without its exciting moments. Just after sunset, every animal within twenty miles of Mystic Knoll had barked, bellowed, howled, hooted, or croaked. Two hours later, hordes of cockroaches had swarmed out of the bathroom plumbing. Piper and her sisters had brushed their teeth with bottled water.

Three hours ago, when Piper had come down to relieve Paige, Harriet had suddenly started scratching, as though plagued by fleas. She had gouged her arm with a talon-toe, drawing blood before Piper could act. She had frozen Harriet and unfrozen her—twice—before the Mystic Knoll effect had run its course.

Leo thought the bizarre animal behaviors were caused by free magic interacting with, rather than being independent of, electromagnetic forces at Mystic Knoll. He believed the configuration of the stones attracted magical power *and* manipulated natural energies. The dual aspect of the stones and their resulting phenomena were probably unique in the world.

"The just-before-dawn shift has arrived." Phoebe walked in with a mug of hot coffee and her paperback novel. "There's more coffee in the big urn if you want some. I just made it."

"After being awake half the night?" Piper shook her head. "Don't think so."

"Anything to report?" Phoebe asked, sitting down.

"Harriet had an itch. It passed." Piper held up

the diary. "Abigail's spell book was interesting, though. Except for the fact that she was a deranged homicidal maniac, some of her early spells and assumptions are amusing. You'll get a kick out of it."

"It's four o'clock in the morning," Phoebe said. "Cliffs Notes version. *Phantom Fire* just started getting good."

"How can you read thrillers when we're always living one?" Piper asked.

"It's fun when it's not real," Phoebe explained.

"I guess." Piper thumbed through the diary to give Phoebe a quick rundown of the contents. "Abigail's first spells were simple manipulations of the elements. She made a creek run dry, melted a bicycle, stuff like that. Mostly to see if she could."

"Like a hobby," Phoebe said.

"Basically." Piper nodded. "At first, just being able to do magic made up for being the ugly kid everyone teased."

"And then?" Phoebe asked.

"And then she got older, smarter, more powerful, and became the primary target of typical teen torture," Piper said. "But Abigail wasn't a typical teen. She learned to refine her spells for specific individuals and results. Rotting Gretchen's teeth and making Karen Stark go bald, for example."

"And Mr. Nestor's dead flowers," Phoebe added.

Piper nodded. The flower incident was mentioned in the diary. "All her revenge spells were annotated with the identity of her victim, what they did to her, what she did to them."

Phoebe raised an eyebrow. "Lucas?"

"His name is on a blank page right before the page with the spell to curse Harriet." Piper pointed to the verse. "No notes, but at least we have the spell."

"That's not much help," Phoebe said. "I heard the spell in my vision."

"And saw the ritual." Piper closed the book and dropped it on the table. "So you're elected to write a reversal spell."

"Okay." Phoebe put her coffee and book on the lamp-table and reached for the diary.

A ticking sound caught Piper's attention. "What's that?"

"What?" Phoebe frowned. "I don't hear anything."

"That scratching sound." Piper glanced around the darkened room, trying to pinpoint the noise.

The sound traveled up the wall by the closet and across the ceiling. Piper's breath caught in her throat when she looked up. A mouse peeked out from a hole at the base of a broken fan fixture in the ceiling. She jumped off her chair when it dropped.

It fell on Phoebe's head.

"What? What is that?" A cry lodged in

Phoebe's throat as she sprang to her feet and frantically shook her head. "Piper! Something's clawing my scalp!"

And nibbling your hair, Piper thought.

"Do something!" Phoebe demanded. She jumped up and down, trying to dislodge the terrified mouse.

"Stand still!" Piper ordered.

"What—" Ida sat bolt upright.

Phoebe squeezed her eyes closed, and Piper flicked her hands to freeze the rodent. She was so tired and stressed, Phoebe and the mouse were lucky it didn't explode.

"What's wrong?" Ida asked. "Harriet—"

"She's fine. Don't move, Phoebe." Piper walked over and parted Phoebe's hair.

"Don't worry." Phoebe winced as Piper picked the mouse up by the tail. Then she opened one eye. "A mouse? There was a mouse in my hair?"

"I've got it. I just don't know what to do with it."

Piper spotted a metal waste can by the desk that would hold the captured critter. As she walked toward it, a sound like a heavy rain rose from the walls, the ceiling, and the floor.

"More company?" Phoebe asked with a worried glance around the room. She jumped onto Piper's chair, out from under the broken fan, as dozens of gray mice invaded the room.

Ida clutched her frayed blanket to her chin.

The small rodents darted from unnoticed holes in the woodwork and under the furniture. They squeezed through a grate in the floor, and more popped out of the ceiling hole above Phoebe's chair.

Piper dropped the frozen mouse and lunged for the desk under the heavily draped window. She changed her mind when mice poured out from under the windowsill. On an intellectual level, she knew it was ridiculous to be squeamish about mice after the horrors she had seen and vanquished. On a more primal level, she couldn't help it.

When a mouse ran over her shoe, Piper squealed and dove for Ida's bed.

Harriet, taking her cues from the same source as the mice, scrambled out of bed and stumbled around the room. The click of her talons was lost in the scurry of a thousand tiny mouse claws racing across the floor. Noses and whiskers twitching, the mice ran in frantic circles. A few rushed the bed and tried to climb the bedspread.

"Freeze them, Piper!" Phoebe shouted.

Piper froze everything in the room except her sister. "Now what?" she asked. The hardwood floor had vanished under a carpet of fur and pink noses.

"I don't know." Phoebe flicked a frozen mouse off the chair with her shoe. "But it's easier to think if they're not moving."

"Yeah," Piper agreed, "but if they're not

moving, they can't leave." Every time an eruption of aberrant animal behavior had occurred, the beasts had reverted to normal within a few minutes.

Phoebe scowled. "Well, then—unfreeze them."

"What about Harriet?" Piper asked. The young woman stood about three feet from the end of her bed.

"Don't look at me." Phoebe raised her hands. "I'm not walking on furry things to get over there."

Piper unfroze the old woman on the bed beside her. "We need to get Harriet onto the bed, Ida. Can you hold her?"

Ida let go of her blanket and nodded. "I'll try."

Piper moved mouse bodies aside with her shoe to clear a spot on the floor. She put her foot down, reached for Harriet's arm, and unfroze her. As Harriet's forward momentum resumed, Piper pulled her onto the bed. Ida flung herself on top of the younger woman.

"Hurry," Ida said, struggling to hold Harriet down.

"Okay—" When Piper set the scene back in motion, Harriet suddenly stopped flailing, and the mice ran back into the walls. A few slowpokes scrambled for cover under the chest of drawers. Another mouse hit the wall. It paused, looking slightly dazed, then disappeared behind a loose flap of wallpaper.

"Are they gone?" Phoebe scanned the floor.

"All except"—Piper cringed when a disoriented mouse leaped off the lamp-table onto Phoebe's jeans—"that one."

"Off! Get off!" Phoebe shook her leg until the little beast dropped to the floor and ran for its life.

"Such a fuss." Ida smoothed Harriet's tangled hair back. "Over a poor little mouse."

Piper's heart went out to the old woman. Not knowing whether Harriet would survive the next day had to be agonizing. Even so, Piper felt no guilt over the fact that her son wouldn't be at risk when the moon eclipsed the sun. Right after breakfast Leo and Wyatt would be off to visit the Elders, far away from Cairn, New Hampshire, and Abigail Thornwood's vendetta.

"Morning!" Nathaniel walked through the back door into the Yankee Bear kitchen.

"What are you doing here?" Ida asked.

Paige was getting a cup of coffee to take back to Harriet's room. Leo had left with Wyatt an hour earlier. Once Paige took over the guard duty, Phoebe wanted to get some more sleep. They had to be as rested as possible for the eclipse that afternoon.

"I gave you the day off for a reason, Nathaniel." Ida tried to shoo him back out the door. "I don't want you here today."

Nathaniel balked when he noticed Paige.

"You're still here?" The question was an accusation.

His shock and suspicion didn't surprise Paige. Since Ida hadn't let anyone stay at the Yankee Bear during the new moon in twenty years, Nathaniel's reaction wasn't unreasonable.

"What? You're not glad to see me?" Paige deliberately acted flippant. One way or another, she had to get Nathaniel far away from the inn. He cared about Harriet, who was getting progressively more restless and difficult to keep quiet and contained.

"Did they threaten to sue if you made them leave?" Nathaniel turned worried blue eyes on Ida.

"Oh, don't be a jerk." Ida gave him a gentle push. "Go home. Go fishing. Just go."

"C'mon, Nathaniel." Paige grabbed a biscuit and walked toward the door. "I'll see you out."

Nathaniel hesitated until Ida threw him a what-are-you-waiting-for look. "So why are you still here?" he asked, following Paige out the door.

"We wanted to be here for the eclipse." Paige hated lying, so she avoided outright fibbing by becoming adept at misleading with the truth to mask her Charmed identity. She backed up her excuse with another fact Piper had learned at the bookstore. "All the other rooms in town are booked."

"Right." Nathaniel frowned. "What time is the eclipse?"

"Two seventeen this afternoon," Paige said as they reached the truck.

Nathaniel nodded. "I just don't understand why Ida—"

Paige cut him off. "She didn't want to spoil our vacation. Total solar eclipses don't happen every day."

"True enough." Nathaniel folded his arms and leaned on the truck fender. "The last one around here was twenty years ago."

Time to change the subject, Paige thought. Nathaniel looked like he was settling in for a conversation she didn't want to have—at least not right now.

It was past nine, and Paige had promised to look over Phoebe's reversal spell. However, they would have to cast it at Mystic Knoll under less than ideal circumstances. Abigail's curse had two integral parts: the original spell in 1985 and the spell Harriet would use to activate the curse during the afternoon eclipse. Consequently they couldn't reverse the curse until the spell was complete, after the transformation had begun.

"What are you doing here on your day off?" Paige asked.

"I wanted to borrow Ida's plumbing tools," Nathaniel explained. "My apartment is in an old converted house down on Pine Crest. None of the tenants are rich, and the drains in all four units are clogged with cockroaches. Just thought I'd save everyone a few bucks."

"I don't think Ida would mind if you used her tools," Paige said.

"Probably not," Nathaniel said. "Be right back."

While she waited for Nathaniel to get back from the shed, Paige glanced toward the woods that separated the Yankee Bear from Mystic Knoll. A flickering sheen drifted through the dense forest.

Lightning bugs or fox fire lichen? Whatever had created the phenomenon, Paige was pretty sure it wasn't *normally* visible during the day.

When Harriet went wild with no warning, Phoebe couldn't orb away or freeze to control her.

"Harriet!" Phoebe exploded off the chair when the woman dashed toward the window. "Stop!"

Strong and sturdy to begin with, Harriet's power and ability were enhanced by the alterations in her biological matrix. Over the past two decades, three days per month, her body had undergone conditioning to facilitate the final transformation. Phoebe's martial-arts skills and rigorous training were useless against her.

"Paige!" Phoebe yelled as she grabbed the loose folds of Harriet's nightdress. "Piper!"

They had agreed to meet at one o'clock, more than an hour before the eclipse. Since Harriet had to be at Mystic Knoll to complete the curse, it logically followed that Abigail had encoded into the spell a compulsion to go there. The plan was fairly straightforward: After Harriet left the Yankee Bear, Paige would orb them all into the large cavern to wait for her. As soon as Harriet began to change, they would use the Power of Three to reverse the curse.

Compared with many of their schemes to get the bad guys, it should have been a snap. Except that Harriet had moved the schedule up twenty minutes.

"Paige!" Phoebe called, digging in her heels to hold Harriet back.

Operating under Abigail's influence, the cursed woman had only one priority: Nothing would stop her from going to Mystic Knoll.

So why am I trying? Phoebe realized she was still protecting Harriet when she had to let her go.

Harriet ripped her nightdress free of Phoebe's grasp. As Phoebe staggered back, Harriet grabbed her arm, yanked her off her feet, and sent her sprawling across the room.

Phoebe lay in a dazed heap, watching as Harriet pulled the drapes off the rods. Paige orbed in just as the young woman crashed through the window.

"Is Harriet okay?" Phoebe asked, drawing herself to her knees. "What's she doing?"

Paige glanced out the window before giving Phoebe a hand up. "She's headed for the woods."

"Then we'd better leave now." Phoebe rubbed a sore muscle in her arm. "Where's Piper?"

"Right here." Piper walked in the bedroom door.

Ida followed her inside. "She's gone?"

"Yes," Phoebe said. They had been over everything with Harriet's grandmother. There was nothing more to say.

Phoebe checked her back pockets for the written spell and a small flashlight, precautions in case they forgot the words in the dark cave. "Ready?"

"Let's do it." Paige took Phoebe and Piper by the hand and orbed.

No matter how many times Paige turned her into a zillion particles of magical light, Phoebe would never get used to the sensation. During the transition, she was a spark of eternity and infinity—of everything and nothing. And then she was herself again.

They materialized at the mouth of the tunnel that opened into the main chamber inside Mystic Knoll.

"Whoa!" Piper looked around the underground rock chamber. Her expression and tone held the same awe Phoebe had felt seeing the glowing cavern the first time in her vision. "I didn't realize it was so big."

"Pretty impressive." Paige nodded.

Being on the site instead of viewing it in her

mind entirely changed Phoebe's perspective. During the vision she had known that the cavern was magnificent. However, the flat ritual stone in the center of the chamber and the three evenly spaced stalagmites were more massive than she had realized. The irregular shape of the cavern, combined with shadow and lichen light, camouflaged an extensive network of alcoves, crevices, and narrow passageways to smaller caves.

But she didn't have time to gawk. "We'd better postpone the sightseeing," Phoebe said. "We know Harriet will get here before the eclipse. We just don't know how long before."

"She'll need time to collect free magic," Piper said, "or her spell won't work."

They had discussed trying to prevent Harriet from gathering the magic she needed to cast the spell, but they had decided against it. Although it might keep the beast from emerging, Harriet would still be cursed, living a dismal, unbearable existence until the next solar eclipse. And Ida wouldn't be around forever to protect and care for her.

Letting the process play out was the only way to save everyone and thwart Abigail.

"Where should we hide?" Piper asked.

Phoebe shrugged as she surveyed the cavern. They had to confront the creature to recite the reversal spell, but it was foolish to endanger themselves before they had to. They wanted to watch from the wings while Harriet chanted her solo.

"What about over there?" Paige pointed to a large outcropping where the cavern wall bulged inward.

An alcove, formed by the outcropping and a deep depression in the back wall, was not glowing with lichen. The pocket was positioned midway between the magical stalagmite behind the flat center stone and the one in front of the flat stone to the right. From her vision, Phoebe knew they would be standing on Harriet's right. Harriet would be facing the main entrance into the cavern, looking between the two forward cones. The Charmed Ones could hug the shadowed alcove wall without being seen, while having an unobstructed view and easy access when they needed to perform the spell.

"It smells like compost in here," Piper whispered as they cut across the floor.

"Just don't sneeze," Phoebe said. "What're all these papery things on the floor?"

"Snake skins," Paige hissed.

The discussion ended there as Piper and Paige stepped into the depression in the back wall. Phoebe pressed into the corner of the outcropping and tried to track the time. The passing minutes seemed like an eternity while they waited, but when Harriet limped out of the tunnel, it felt like no time had passed.

Harriet moved along the far wall, a shadow only partially visible in the biolight, threading a path through stalagmites and boulders.

As Phoebe watched, she thought her breathing was too loud and that Harriet could surely sense that she and her sisters were there to thwart Abigail's plan. And it wouldn't be easy. Even now, before the final stage of transformation had begun, the woman exuded a terrifying primal power.

Hidden in the dark space, Piper and Paige were so still that Phoebe would have felt completely alone if not for the Charmed compact that bound them. They all tensed when Harriet turned abruptly and hobbled to the center of the chamber.

In the glistening glow of illuminated stalactites above, additional changes in her appearance were evident as she climbed onto the ritual stone. In place of Harriet's tangled hair, a crest of bone formed a ridge over the crown of her head and down her neck. Yellow, reptilian eyes gleamed with predatory disdain. Bony spikes protruded from her shoulders, and loose skin hung from her arms.

Phoebe breathed in deeply, slowly, steeling herself for the task ahead. Piper found her sisters' hands in the dark and squeezed them for luck. Feeling the Power of Three bolstered their confidence.

As Harriet stood, silent and unmoving, on the raised slab, she showed no sign of knowing she had company. After several more minutes she closed her double-lidded lizard eyes. Somehow

she knew that the moon had begun to pass
between Earth and the sun.

At first the humming sound in Harriet's
throat was almost inaudible. But as the sound
grew louder, the stale air in the cavern com-
pressed.

Phoebe's ears reacted to an increased pressure she hadn't detected in her vision. She felt as
though she had been suddenly submerged in the
depths of the ocean.

Paige inhaled, and Piper clamped her hands
to the sides of her head.

Then red sparks snapped through the barrier between the magical ether and Earthly
reality.

Every burst of magic felt like a needle of fire
in Phoebe's stomach, then molten knives when
the sparks elongated into bolts. Booms and
cracks sent tremors through the rock as each
fragment of free magic broke through the invisible boundary. Flaring bolts arrowed through the
cavern, rebounded off walls, and crackled as
they were swept into a swirl.

Phoebe's head spun and her stomach
churned as ribbons of red streaked past. The
flow shifted in an instant. Instead of a circular
pattern, the streams traveled in straight lines
between the three cones anchored to the floor.
Holding her ears against the pressure, Phoebe
suddenly imagined she was being pulled into
the maelstrom.

"Phoebe—" Piper murmured her name, but Phoebe was too stunned to respond. She *was* being pulled into the speeding stream of crimson magic.

"What's happening?" Paige's voice betrayed uncertainty and fear.

"Not sure." Phoebe turned, grabbing at the rock wall and finding nothing to hold on to. As her feet began to slide out from under her, she realized something they had overlooked: The chamber absorbed and amplified magic.

Using a power inherited from or instilled by Abigail, Harriet was drawing free magic into the chamber. Magic contained in artifacts or possessed by beings was not affected. *Usually not affected*, Phoebe thought. They were at ground zero, directly in line with two of the cones that absorbed magic!

"We're right in the path of the receptors!" Phoebe had to yell to be heard over the thunderous booms. Harriet was too immersed in the ritual to notice them now.

"Mystic Knoll is going to absorb our magic?" Piper was aghast and angry.

"No, I don't think so!" Remembering how the cones absorbed magic in her vision, Phoebe was pretty sure Mystic Knoll couldn't ingest them. Since the pull was getting stronger, she hoped her deductions were right. "We're being attracted! Like iron filings to a magnet!"

"I can't hang onnnnnn—" As Paige was

whipped into the magical flow, the sound of her voice hung over Phoebe for a second. Phoebe thought she saw a white orb sparkle, but it vanished almost as soon as it appeared.

"Phoebeeeeee—" Piper shouted as she entered the stream. She flicked her hands to freeze, but nothing happened.

Uh-oh, Phoebe thought as she was grabbed by the stream. Had their powers just been temporarily neutralized, or were they gone for good?

Zipping by rock walls and under pointed stalactites, Phoebe couldn't concentrate on anything except what was happening at the moment. And everything was happening at blinding speed. She was not aware of breathing, and all her senses but sight had been suppressed. Hurtling toward the forward wall, she tensed in anticipation of a bone-crunching collision. But the stream made a hard left, carrying her with it.

Several ribbons of red split off toward the forward cone to the left of the ritual slab. As Phoebe sped by, she realized that Paige was flattened against it. Paige winced as bolts of red magic struck the stalactite around her. The fragments were quickly absorbed.

The cone behind the center stone slab where Harriet stood had captured Piper.

Phoebe braced for impact as she zoomed toward the third cone at the front of the cavern. A passive passenger in the stream, she couldn't extricate herself or alter her course. The wind was knocked out of her as she slammed into the hard conical receptacle. A blaze of incoming red engulfed her, and she flinched as spear after scarlet spear hit the cone. She couldn't move or speak. She could only watch and listen when the conical traps pulsed, and Harriet began to chant.

> *"Cast from creatures of the night,*
> *Fang and claw, leather and flight . . ."*

Harriet's voice resonated in the massive cave, gaining intensity as she drew strength from the stones. Incorporated into the ancient mechanism, Phoebe convulsed with each phrase spoken. The stones amplified the power within her and her sisters, adding it to the free magic the cones radiated toward the center stone.

> *"Two times ten has passed, the core*
> *Of her vengeance waits no more."*

The pulsations in the cones didn't abate as the last word echoed down the corridors of the Mystic Knoll maze. Residual threads of red static continued to skim the surface of the cones.

Held fast to the stalagmite, Phoebe fought nausea and weakness to witness the insidious events Abigail had instigated so long ago. Piper and Paige hung like rag dolls on the other two receptors. She had no doubt her sisters were also watching and waiting, hoping for a chance to execute the reversal spell.

Atop the flat stone, Harriet Thornwood changed into a mythical creature brought to life by her mother's depraved spell.

Harriet's human face elongated into a knobby shape that was a cross between a dragon and a seahorse. The ridge on her head grew outward, then flattened and fanned into a saurian crest. Smaller bony plates covered her lengthening neck. Arms thickened and grew longer with scales replacing skin. Hands and fingernails morphed into shortened forefeet and claws. As her legs muscled up into power-ful hindquarters, her tail grew out. The bony protrusions on her shoulders transformed into the supporting structures of ribbed, leathery wings.

The shreds of Harriet's nightdress fluttered to the floor as the beast rose on huge hind legs and roared.

The entire transformation had taken less than two minutes.

Phoebe cringed as the creature's massive tail whipped from side to side. The motion gener-ated a gale-force wind that howled through the cavern in an erratic frenzy, turning snake skins to dust.

Like it wants to get out, Phoebe thought, fight-ing to stay conscious.

The ferocious roar of the beast and the battering wind shook the bedrock foundation of the chamber. Each roar and movement of wing and tail caused more damage. Rock walls cracked. Stalactites were shaken loose to shatter on the floor. Patches of glowing lichen dimmed as boulders shifted and parts of the ceiling caved in.

Phoebe had faced death too many times not to be prepared for a premature but inevitable end. But she didn't want to die, bound and helpless, under tons of rock.

The beast screamed.

The wind shrieked.

And the roof of Mystic Knoll's main chamber blew away.

Chapter

10

Paige was furious, sick to her stomach, drained of energy—and maybe even her magic—and stuck to stone! She'd had bad days before, but this one ranked with the worst.

Especially if I end up buried alive or dead, she thought with a glance upward.

When the walls of the cave began to crumble, she expected the ceiling to come down. Instead a large hole was blown in the top of the cavern with such force, most of the debris rained on the surrounding area. Paige was so elated to have escaped being crushed, she almost didn't mind smashing into the rock floor.

One second she was plastered against a stalagmite that doubled as a free magic amplifier, and the next she was flat on her face on the ground.

Paige rolled onto her back just in time to see Harriet—or the thing that used to be Harriet—

fly through the opening with a defiant roar. The beat of huge wings created massive air currents. Dislodged pebbles cascaded into the cavern.

Paige barely felt the bits of stone that pelted her face. They had lost their Innocent. She could think of nothing else.

"Is anybody else sore, mortified, and thoroughly irate?" Piper asked, groaning.

"Yes." Gritting her teeth, Paige slowly got to her feet. Her legs were wobbly, and a dizzy spell threatened her balance. She closed her eyes and breathed deeply until her equilibrium was restored.

Phoebe hurried toward them from the cone that had held her with its magical forces. She limped slightly, holding her hand over her thigh.

"What happened?" Piper brushed dust and crushed rock off her arms.

"I was skewered by a stalactite." Phoebe held up the pointed shard that had impaled her leg. "But we've got worse things than my flesh wound to worry about."

Paige nodded. "We lost an Innocent, and now she's the enemy."

"Let's not be too hasty here," Phoebe said. "Based on what we've seen of evil before, I'm willing to bet Harriet's innocence won't be lost until she kills somebody. We can still save her."

"If we can catch her," Piper said. She examined a bruise on her forearm, then looked up, giving Phoebe her full attention.

"Okay, how do you hunt down a giant bat-lizard?" Paige asked.

"Beats me. I don't think anyone's wanted to try before," Phoebe said. "But we have no choice."

"Plus we have this nifty spell that will go to waste if we don't find her!" Paige knew she was making a feeble attempt to keep things more upbeat than she feared they really were. She wanted to believe saving Harriet was possible, but they had to face facts: Success was a long shot. "Okay. So say we find her. How do we get her back here to Mystic Knoll?"

"Do we have to get her back here?" Piper asked.

"I think so," Paige replied. "Abigail used the free magic and amplification power of Mystic Knoll to cast the curse in the first place. Harriet was programmed to use the same forces to finish it."

"Right." Piper folded her arms. "But why would that affect our reversal spell? We have all the magic we need."

"Maybe not," Paige said. "What if Harriet the beast is magically stronger than she should be because while Mystic Knoll had us pinned, it put the Power of Three in the magical mix?"

Piper's eyes widened. "So to change her back, the Power of Three needs a Mystic Knoll boost too?"

"I hate to say it, but that makes sense,"

Phoebe said. "There's still magic in the cones."

Paige glanced at the nearest stalagmite receptacle. Streaks of bright red flared against a muted red glow. "Leftovers?"

"Could be," Phoebe said. "With our magic added in, the site had way more than necessary to complete the spell."

Paige frowned. "But how do we access it without becoming the main attraction again?"

"Balance," Piper said. "We have two major forces of magic, us and Mystic Knoll. There has to be a position within the configuration where both forces will combine without one overpowering the other."

"Great." Phoebe raised a quizzical eyebrow. "Where?"

"I'm working on it," Piper said.

"I don't think we've got an open window for doing this spell," Paige said. "Eventually the magic in the cones will leak away. So the sooner we get Harriet or the creature or whatever back here, the better."

"How are we supposed to do that?" Piper asked. "I'm fresh out of mythical beastie kibble."

"Bait," Phoebe said. "Abigail created the beast for one purpose—to get revenge on her enemies and their children."

"That might work." Piper rubbed the purplish bruise on her arm. "Abigail had a lot of people on her hit list. We should be able to convince a few of them to come here."

"I'm on it," Phoebe said. "But I'll have to go back to the Yankee Bear."

"I'll look for Harriet." Paige looked up at the sky. "I don't know if I'll find her, but I'll try—our spell won't matter if she kills someone. Or something."

"Our spell won't work unless I find out how to tap Mystic Knoll's magic without it killing us!" Piper exclaimed. "I'll stay here and try to figure it out."

"Better orb me back to the inn before you take off after Harriet, Paige," Phoebe said. "I don't have time to waste walking."

After she dropped Phoebe on the edge of the Yankee Bear property, Paige surprisingly had no trouble tracking the beast, despite its head start. She orbed into a tall tree, then followed the swath of broken treetops the creature had left in its windy wake. At the edge of the woods she plotted a course over flattened crops, fences, and through another extensive stand of woods. The beast's flight path angled away from town, but it was too direct to be random. The creature knew where it was going.

Orbing from tree to tree, Paige pursued the beast through dense forest and up the side of a mountain. When she caught up, the creature was circling a lookout tower that forest rangers used to spot fires. The tower reminded her of a notation in Abigail's diary.

In the third grade, before her abilities emerged,

a little boy named Dennis Flynn had plagued
Abigail with typical pranks and taunts. Dennis
had called her names, ignored her, and dumped
her cafeteria tray, among other childish offenses.
She slipped off his radar in fourth grade, but
Abigail never forgot. Her first revenge spell had
turned Dennis Flynn's lucky baseball bat into
sawdust. And according to Abigail's notes, from
age nine on, Dennis had wanted to be a forest
ranger.

The creature screeched and buzzed the top of
the fire tower. The structure was a series of plat-
forms connected by open staircases. The top
floor was enclosed by a four-foot-high wall and
capped with a peaked roof. Shingles and
wooden steps were torn off by the wind as the
beast flew by. The corner struts snapped. Since
its prey wasn't inside the tower, the enraged
creature screamed and moved on. The wooden
lookout post crumbled as Paige orbed after the
beast.

The new course followed a narrow river that
wound around the mountain, through a wooded
valley, and into a large fenced pasture. The wind
created by massive wings churned the creek into
a torrent of white-water rapids. A herd of horses
raced for safety as the creature passed overhead.
Spotting the roof of an isolated farmhouse, Paige
wondered if Laurel Savarin was the next target.

Laurel's entry in Abigail's diary had been
notated with a star. An accomplished equestrian

and straight-A student, Laurel had organized a schoolwide shunning of Abigail that had lasted weeks in their junior year of high school. Soon after, Laurel had scored below average on her college entrance SATs and fallen off her horse in every jumping trial at a regional horse show.

The house had been built on a dead-end dirt road, several hundred yards from a paved country highway. A barn was connected to the two-story farmhouse by a long wooden passageway. The passageway provided protection from severe winter weather. Paige couldn't tell if anyone was home until the creature blasted the brick chimney with its tail. A woman inside the house screamed. The floors shook as Paige orbed into a bedroom on the second floor. On the creature's next pass, something crashed on the lower level, but there was no scream.

Paige tiptoed to the top of the stairs. A middle-age woman lay on the floor in a puddle of water. Pieces of a broken vase and flowers were scattered around her. She was out cold.

When the beast grazed the side of the house, plaster fell from the ceiling and knickknacks rattled on tables. The creature landed outside the front door with a resounding boom, shaking the building and cracking the walls. A framed collection of horse-show ribbons hung on the wall beside Paige. A brass plate on the wooden frame identified Laurel Savarin as the 1981 Junior

Jumper Champion. The framed piece fell, but didn't break.

Paige orbed downstairs, knelt beside the unconscious woman, and orbed her out just as the creature obliterated the front porch and rammed the house. They materialized on the edge of the pasture by the woods, where Paige could watch the beast. She suspected it could sense the people Abigail had targeted, and she tensed to orb again. The beast, however, seemed to be growing more frenzied and less focused. After it demolished the front of the house and discovered the prey was gone, it flew off, roaring in frustrated anger.

Anger or hunger? Paige wondered. Harriet had used enormous energies to become the beast, and then had expended more, hunting without success.

When Laurel moaned, Paige orbed her home and put the woman back on the floor where she had collapsed. Laurel would never know what had happened to her house or how she had survived.

Paige took to the trees again, wondering how to feed the beast without serving up Abigail's old classmates. Eating might postpone the inevitable kill that would destroy Harriet's chance for salvation. If Paige could, she had to buy time while Piper and Phoebe prepared to lure the beast back to Mystic Knoll.

Still tracking the creek, the beast's route took

it deeper into the wilderness to a small lake. Paige watched from her perch in a tall pine as the creature executed a monster-style cannon-ball. When it hit, the water level in the lake dropped several feet. Water shot a hundred feet into the air and a wave washed a hundred yards into the woods. Hundreds of fish were stranded on dry land when the water receded back into the lake.

When the beast began to gobble its catch, Paige took advantage of the break to orb back to the inn.

Ida was sitting on the front porch, waiting, when Phoebe returned. Phoebe did not mince words. She told the old woman everything, but she made no excuses for why they had failed to save Harriet. When she finished, Ida just sat, staring down the driveway.

Watching the grieving grandmother digest the news was one of the harder things Phoebe had done lately. Regardless of the problems Ida had faced raising her cursed granddaughter, Harriet had been—*was*—her joy and reason for living. To lose her was more than the old woman could bear. The light in Ida's dark eyes, icy with suspicion when Phoebe first met her, had brightened with hope when it seemed there might be a chance to save Harriet and now began to dim. That was more than Phoebe could bear.

"It's not over." Phoebe gently gripped Ida's

arms and stared into her pain. "We still have a chance to save her."

"Too late." Ida shook her head. "Abigail always wins. Always."

"Not this time." Phoebe's eyes flashed. "I mean it, Ida. We can beat Abigail, but I need your help."

Ida frowned, searching Phoebe's face for the lie that wasn't there. "I don't believe you can save Harriet, but"—she sighed, then shrugged. "But I know you think you can, and I think you have to try. So, yes. I'll help."

"That's all I wanted to hear." Phoebe smiled. "I'll get the diary and meet you in the kitchen."

Ignoring the throb in her injured thigh, Phoebe dashed into Harriet's room and grabbed the blue book off the lamp-table. As she turned to leave, she realized that the drapes and rods had been put back over the broken window. The rollaway was gone, and Harriet's bed had been made with fresh linens and a blanket that wasn't torn.

Denial or acceptance? Phoebe wondered. Ida had fixed up the room before she knew Harriet's fate, but whether she had expected the best or the worst, love had dictated her actions. Although there were serious exceptions, most of the people who wrote to "Ask Phoebe" wanted advice about trivial, ridiculous, or selfish problems. They could learn a few things about caring and courage from Ida Thornwood.

Ida had mugs of tea waiting when Phoebe got to the kitchen table. The old woman noticed the blood on her jeans for the first time. "I'll get the first-aid kit."

"It's nothing," Phoebe said, sitting down with the diary.

"Just drink your tea and let me take care of this." Ida got a metal first-aid box from under the sink. She set it on the table, then added a clean dishcloth, a pan of hot water, and a bottle of hydrogen peroxide.

Phoebe talked while Ida tended her injury.

"All the people Abigail wrote about in her diary are targets," Phoebe said. "We don't need everyone for our plan to work, just enough to make Mystic Knoll irresistible to the—Harriet."

"Um-hmm." Ida cut Phoebe's jeans and poured hydrogen peroxide into the exposed wound. The oxygen fluid bubbled, killing any bacteria.

Phoebe had mentally compiled a list of the people she and her sisters had met or heard about. She pulled a pen from the jar, ripped a sheet of paper off a note pad by the phone, and wrote the list. "Does Gretchen have any kids?"

Ida shook her head. "Never married. No children."

"Karen Stark . . . ," Phoebe went on.

"Karen's brother owns Stark's Pharmacy," Ida said. "Her daughter, Nancy, works there."

"Oh, right. I met Nancy." Phoebe wrote down the names of the women. Abigail had mentioned the tour guide in the diary because of a squirrel attack. Although Tammy had never done anything to her, Abigail thought she was too nice and too perfect—a phony who deserved to have her hair torn out by the roots. "Brad York's daughter?"

"Molly went to college in Arizona and never came back." Ida placed a gauze pad over the cut.

Phoebe frowned. Abigail had noted that Brad was Molly's father, which made him the parental surrogate for her wrath. Florence Nestor-Haynes's father had yelled at Abigail. He was dead, but his daughter and his grandson, Troy, were at risk. She added their names.

"Will you ask Lucas Barnes?" Ida asked without looking up. She taped the gauze pad in place, then enlarged the slit in Phoebe's jeans.

"Yes," Phoebe said. "Lucas is our best chance of luring Harriet back."

Ida nodded and wound a gauze bandage around Phoebe's thigh, under her jeans. "I don't think it would be a good idea to mention this to his wife. Anne is a little touchy about—"

"Harriet?" Phoebe watched as Ida cut the bandage lengthwise, separated the sliced ends, wrapped them around her thigh in opposite directions, and tied them.

"Abigail," Ida said. "Anne is scared to death of Abigail."

"Understood." Phoebe counted the names. "Nine. Guess that's it."

"Plus me and old Ned Johnson," Ida said. She took a needle and thread from the kit and stitched Phoebe's cut jeans back together. It was a temporary fix to protect the bandage.

"You're not a target, Ida," Phoebe said. "I'm not sure you understand how dangerous—"

"Doesn't matter," Ida cut her off. "If you get Harriet back, I have to be there, because she trusts me. If you don't—well, then I don't care what happens to me."

Phoebe didn't argue. "Who's Ned Johnson?"

"An old friend," Ida said. "Ned never believed Doc Randall's spider story, and he never forgave Abigail for making his cat's toe fall off. Cat's dead now, but he still wants to get back at her."

"Eleven it is, then," Phoebe opened the phone book.

"And Nathaniel," Ida added. "He's the only other person Harriet trusts—and likes."

"Uh, I'm not sure about Nathaniel, Ida." Phoebe didn't want to refuse Ida or Harriet anything, but she might not have a choice. "Paige said that Nathaniel doesn't believe in the paranormal, and he has no patience for people who do."

"Yes, I know," Ida said.

Phoebe pressed gently. "And we are dealing with some super-paranormal stuff here."

Ida almost smiled. "I hired Nathaniel *because*

he's so positive that what he believes is right. He's so sure, he won't believe his own eyes, even if he sees something that proves what he believes is wrong. Like Harriet with fangs or scales."

Phoebe knew from her psychology studies and her mail at the *Bay Mirror* that the trait Ida described was remarkably common. An astounding number of people simply did not let facts get in the way of their beliefs.

"All right." Phoebe flipped though the phone book to "N." There was one listing under "F." Nestor-Haynes. She dialed. "Florence? This is Phoebe Halliwell, from San Francisco. I'm sorry to bother you on a Sunday—"

"No bother, Phoebe," Florence said. "Troy and I just came in from watching the eclipse."

"Cool." Phoebe got right to the point. "Since you run the local newspaper, I thought you'd probably want to be at Mystic Knoll this afternoon. Troy, too."

"What's up?" Florence asked, intrigued.

"For one thing, there's a big hole in the top of the main cavern," Phoebe said. "For another, we're going to realign the electromagnetic field to stop all the freaky animal uprisings and other miscellaneous weirdness that happens around here."

Ida kept sewing, but she was listening intently.

"You're kidding," Florence said. "I won't

have anything interesting to write about." The editor-publisher paused. "You're not kidding. When?"

"As soon as you can get there. Wait for me in the parking lot." Phoebe hung up and opened the book to "B" for "Barnes." At least it was Sunday, when most people were home. As she started to dial, Paige sauntered in the back door.

"Where's—" Phoebe let the unfinished question hang in the air. Paige was supposed to be keeping an eye on the beast.

"Lunching on sushi at a little lake in the mountains," Paige said.

"She didn't—" Phoebe didn't want to mention the no-killing rule in front of Ida.

Paige shook her head. "No, just a close call, so I don't want to be gone too long. How're you doing?"

"We're on it." Phoebe picked up the list and looked at Ida. "I have to talk to Paige about something. Could you call a couple of these people?"

"Everyone in town thinks I'm nuts." Ida knotted and cut the thread, then took the list. "But I guess I can talk to Ned and Nathaniel."

Paige's head snapped toward Phoebe, and she mouthed Nathaniel's name in disbelief.

Phoebe scowled a warning at Paige and glanced at Ida.

The old woman had a point. Phoebe had met Florence at the *Cairn Clarion*, so she wasn't a total stranger. Appealing to the editor's journalistic instincts had made Florence an easy sell. But what if Abigail's other victims didn't want to get involved with her reclusive mother? Especially in some harebrained scheme to alter the electromagnetic nature of an ancient mystical site?

"And Lucas. I can talk to Lucas." Ida took a deep breath. "But what if he won't come?"

"Tell him this is his only chance to get payback on Abigail," Phoebe said, "and his last chance to help his daughter."

"Don't worry, Ida," Paige said. "If you and Phoebe can't convince Lucas to come on his own, I can always orb him."

"Just get Ned and Lucas and his son, Ida. I'll take care of the rest, including Nathaniel." Phoebe had an idea, but first she had an errand for Paige. She motioned her sister into the front foyer. "I need the crystals to make a cage."

"To trap Harriet," Paige said.

"Yes, and to keep our other twelve Innocents safe," Phoebe said. "But as far as our guests and Nathaniel are concerned, we're using the crystals to alter the electromagnetic dynamic at Mystic Knoll."

"And why are we inviting Nathaniel?" Paige asked with a hint of annoyance.

"Ida insisted." Phoebe shrugged.

"I'll get the crystals." Paige rolled her eyes as she orbed out.

When Phoebe got back to the kitchen, Ida was still on the phone.

"Yes, it will be good to see you again too, Ned." Ida's sad smile suddenly changed into an amused look of shock. "Stop that! You haven't changed in sixty years, you old scoundrel. No wonder Ms. Stinkle made you stand in the corner every day."

"Sounds like somebody had a crush on Ida," Phoebe teased.

"Ancient history." Ida held up the list. "Ned is going to call Brad. They're fishing buddies, and Ned won't take no for an answer."

"Excellent," Phoebe said. "And Lucas?"

"He'll be there with Tim." Ida fought back a tear. "All I had to say was, 'Harriet needs you.'"

Phoebe gave her a thumbs-up. "So that leaves Karen and Nancy, Gretchen, Tammy, and Nathaniel. I'll need their addresses and phone numbers."

Phoebe dropped off Ida by the Mystic Knoll gift shop. Although groups made her nervous after decades of seclusion, Ida was willing to do anything to help Harriet, including play hostess to several past victims of her daughter's abuse. Phoebe promised to hurry back, and cursed the lack of cell-phone service as she sped toward town.

Nathaniel's apartment house was on the corner of Pine Crest and Lewis Avenue. He was outside tossing Ida's plumbing tools into his truck when Phoebe parked the van.

"Hey there, Phoebe." Nathaniel nodded with a slow frown. "Did you enjoy the eclipse?"

"Uh—" Phoebe's brain stalled. She hadn't actually seen the eclipse because she was underground. "It went off pretty much as I expected."

"Not as exciting as Paige thought it would be, huh?" Nathaniel's obvious irritation shifted to curiosity. "So what brings you out here? Is something wrong at the Yankee Bear?"

Phoebe didn't answer the question. "I have an idea that might jump-start your thesis."

"Really?" Nathaniel leaned on his truck. "That's right. You're a psychologist."

"Yeah." Phoebe launched into the pitch she had rehearsed on the drive into Cairn. "I've been thinking about your premise, about locals believing their legends and how many residents of *this* town want to believe that Mystic Knoll is magic."

Nathaniel nodded. "That's why I'm here."

"In fact," Phoebe said, "they want it so much, they won't let facts interfere with what they think is true."

"I'm listening," Nathaniel said.

Phoebe could tell Nathaniel was intrigued and that he couldn't see that her premise applied to him. But whatever he thought was irrelevant, as long as he agreed to help.

"So I've come up with a field experiment, to see if anybody can be convinced they're wrong," Phoebe said. "Twelve people, mostly believers, and you. Interested?"

"Yeah, but why are you?" Nathaniel asked.

"I'm a psychologist who writes an advice column for a newspaper," Phoebe confessed. She plunged ahead when Nathaniel frowned. "This particular mind-set isn't restricted to people who believe in ghosts or UFOs. All kinds of people ignore facts for all kinds of reasons. I've just never been in a town where half the population adamantly believed in variations of the same fantasy."

"Cairn is distinctive that way." Nathaniel rubbed the dark stubble on his unshaven chin. "It does kind of beg to be explored, doesn't it? What does Paige think?"

Phoebe rolled her eyes to give the impression she and her sister disagreed. "That it's mean to debunk harmless myths. Are you in?"

"Yep," Nathaniel said. "What do you need from me?"

"I need you to call these ladies and convince them to drive out to Mystic Knoll right away." Phoebe handed him the paper with the addresses and phone numbers.

"For what exactly?" Nathaniel asked. "A picnic? Ancient ritual?"

"No." Phoebe's grin betrayed her mischievous nature. "Tell them we're going to realign the electromagnetic patterns at Mystic Knoll so all the crazy stuff will end."

"We are?" Nathaniel laughed. "And you expect these women to buy that?"

"In this town?" Phoebe exaggerated a look of amazement. "Where half the locals think Abigail Thornwood used spells to torment them? Yes! They'll definitely buy it."

Nathaniel hesitated, then nodded. "Only one way to find out. Let's go inside and call."

Phoebe exhaled deeply as she followed Nathaniel up the walk. She didn't have a clue what anyone would believe when the day was over. The only thing that mattered was saving Harriet from her mother's curse.

Piper stepped out of the shadows when Paige orbed into the chamber and placed an armload of crystals and a blue bathrobe on the ritual stone.

"Okay, I understand the crystals." Piper nodded her approval. Trapping the beast would make casting the spell a significantly safer process.

"That was Phoebe's idea," Paige said. "She thinks the free magic in the stones will make the Crystal Cage bigger and strong enough to hold the beast."

"I hope she's right." Piper picked up the bathrobe. "And this?"

"That's my idea," Paige explained. "The beast shredded Harriet's nightdress, so she doesn't have anything to wear when she gets back."

"Good thinking," Piper said. Paige had a knack for details she and Phoebe sometimes missed.

Paige brushed a lock of hair off her face and nodded toward the cones. "Any luck figuring out how to tap into those?"

"Sort of." Piper glanced at the stalagmites. Streaks of red flashed over a reddish glow, but the glow had dimmed. "It kind of depends on your definition of lucky."

"Can we use Mystic Knoll's magic?" Paige asked.

"I think so," Piper said. "But do we want to?"

"Lost me," Paige said.

A demonstration would make the point better, Piper decided. She waved Paige over to a spot midway between the rear cone and the forward-right cone.

"Can you feel it?" Piper asked when Paige was in position.

"What?" Paige asked, puzzled.

"Never mind. You'll know," Piper said. "Move back and forth between the cones. I think the field shifts as the free magic leaks away."

"Okay." Paige moved a few feet to her left.

"Can you feel it now?" Piper asked.

Paige shook her head and moved back the other way. She stopped, hesitated, then stepped back to the left.

"Now?" Piper couldn't keep an edge of frustration out of her voice.

"No, I—" Paige suddenly stiffened, as though she had been struck by a massive dose of electricity. Her eyes widened with astonishment and fear before she tore herself out of the field.

"Guess you felt that," Piper said.

"What was that?" Paige's face was ashen.

"That was an infusion of concentrated, raw magic," Piper explained. It had taken several minutes before the buzzing noise in her head had subsided when she first connected with the field. The effects were staggering, but not debilitating. "I'm glad you're here so we can find out what happens when we increase the Charmed factor by one."

"When both of us are in the field?" Paige asked.

Piper nodded. She wasn't thrilled by the prospect of being zapped by megamagic again. But it was better to find out now if they could take it than to realize they couldn't handle it when the Harriet monster was rampaging around the cavern.

"Here goes." Piper walked across the floor to the area between the rear cone and the forward-left cone. "Ready?"

"No, but a witch has to do what a witch has to do." Inhaling and exhaling slowly, Paige stepped into Mystic Knoll's magical field.

Piper stepped back, then to the side, until she made the connection. The raw magical energy hit with a force she could only equate with being struck by lightning. Every molecule in her body was on fire, every nerve was electrified. Her hair billowed out from the ponytail band, and her

heartbeat boomed in her ears. She tried to
remember the words of Wyatt's favorite nursery
rhyme as practice for the spell.

Wrinkle, starkle, katy diddle . . .

She knew that wasn't right, but her mind
refused to focus. For a moment she was mesmer-
ized by the kaleidoscopic stars twinkling in front
of her eyes.

Out! Piper screamed at herself. With a monu-
mental effort, she lunged forward just far
enough to break the connection. She fell in a
heap, convinced that she and her sisters could
not survive Mystic Knoll's raw power.

Chapter

11

"Okay, everybody!" Phoebe gathered her band of unsuspecting volunteers around the ritual stone.

Nathaniel hung back with Ida, an interested observer, pretending to participate for appearance's sake. He didn't have a clue that the experiment was a front for a magical spell. He was both fascinated and amused that no one had turned down the chance to take part in the pseudoscientific exercise.

If the circumstances weren't so dire, Phoebe would have been fascinated and amused too. Harriet wasn't the only one at risk. Everyone in the cave was in danger, including herself and her sisters. Piper and Paige had discovered that Mystic Knoll amplified their power internally. Their own magic might kill them.

"This is Piper." Phoebe introduced her sister. After Piper and Paige had almost fried themselves with boosted magic, Paige had left to check on the beast. She wouldn't return until it did.

"Hey, Piper!" Brad York waved. "Remember me?"

"Sure do." Piper smiled. "How are those fish doing?"

"They're alive." Brad laughed.

Gretchen was stuffed into jeans and a tank top with her bleached-blond hair pulled back in a large plastic clip. "How long has the hole been in the roof, Tammy?"

"Not long." Tammy shrugged. "It wasn't there Friday."

"How'd it get there?" Troy Haynes asked. He was a basketball player, tall and lanky, with the curiosity of a born newspaperman.

"Caved in, I guess." Tim Barnes cocked his head and nodded as he studied the ceiling. He was a handsome boy with dimples and his father's gray eyes.

Lucas was the only one who didn't look up. His troubled gaze darted around the cavern. He was the only one who knew that Harriet had something to do with what was going on. If Harriet was involved, then Abigail might be too. To his credit, he showed no signs of regret that he had come.

Karen Stark was slim with short dark hair. She wore a ruffled blouse, pleated slacks, and sandals, a classy contrast to her teenage daughter's oversized T-shirt and sweatpants. Nancy's light brown hair was held back by an exercise headband.

"Is it okay if I take notes?" Florence held up a memo pad and pen. She had left her camera and tape recorder in her car at Phoebe's request.

"Yes," Phoebe said, "as long as you don't move once you're in position."

"Just don't quote me, Florence," old Ned Johnson said. Tufts of white hair stuck out from under a blue baseball cap. He wore a plaid flannel shirt over a T-shirt and baggy denim coveralls. The toes of his heavy work boots were scuffed.

"Don't worry, Ned," Florence said. "I won't."

"All right, listen up." Phoebe clapped her hands for attention. "It's absolutely vital that you follow our instructions exactly. We're not messing around here, people. This is a serious experiment."

Everyone nodded with somber expressions.

Phoebe suppressed a pang of guilt. Although Abigail had loosed the creature of vengeance on the town, she had brought twelve Innocents into a deadly situation under false pretenses. They were Innocents by Charmed standards, she realized, but they weren't all entirely innocent. Some were unjustly meant to pay for the sins of their families. A few had been targeted because they had taunted and humiliated Abigail. None of them knew that the real reason for their presence in the cavern was to lure the beast.

Piper had already placed four of the five crystals in deep alcoves and crevices around the perimeter of the cavern. The bait would be split into five groups, each placed beyond the crystals, behind walls of rock, where they wouldn't be able to see what happened in the center of the chamber.

"Ned, you're with Karen and Nancy," Phoebe said. "Piper will show you where to go. Nathaniel, take Ida to that cone"—she pointed to the stalagmite behind the ritual stone—"and wait for me. Brad and Tammy—"

Phoebe faltered when Paige ran out of the tunnel. She had orbed into the passageway to avoid being seen. Paige flapped her arms and gestured toward the hole above to indicate that the creature was en route.

"Brad and Tammy," Phoebe repeated. "With Paige, over there." She pointed and waved, hoping Paige remembered to place the people on the far side of the crystal.

Piper returned to hustle Lucas, Tim, and Gretchen into position. Phoebe took Florence and Troy to an alcove near the spot where she and her sisters had hidden earlier.

"What's that?" Troy asked when he saw the crystal.

"You ask really good questions, Troy," Phoebe said as she pointed the boy and his mother to a spot behind a bank of tall stalagmites. Aware that Troy's inquisitive instincts could get him killed today, she issued a warning. "Stay here with your mom, and I'll answer your questions later. If you don't do what I say, you might not be around later. Got it?"

Florence dropped her notebook and wrapped her arms around her son. "Abigail?"

"Is dead," Phoebe said. She was glad Florence had gotten the message, but she wasn't going on the record. "And she's going to stay that way."

Phoebe rushed back into the center of the chamber. Piper and Paige were standing behind the flat stone, watching the sky.

"Better hurry, Phoebe," Piper said.

"On my way." Phoebe grabbed the fifth crystal off the raised stone and ran for the back wall. Nathaniel and Ida stood by the cone, waiting as she had asked. "You've got to move back, Nathaniel. C'mon."

"I want to watch whatever it is you're going to do to convince these people the electromagnetic character of these stones has changed," Nathaniel said.

Ida cuffed his arm. "You are the most stubborn man I have ever met, Nathaniel Coffey. More than Joshua. He was nasty, but you're just plain pigheaded. Now do as Phoebe says!"

Nathaniel looked stunned as Ida strode toward the back wall.

"Please, Nathaniel," Phoebe pleaded. "Now!"

"They blew the roof off the place," Ida snapped with a quick look back. "What more do you want?"

"We didn't blow the roof off," Phoebe said,

pushing Nathaniel ahead of her. "Not technically."

Phoebe steered them into a deep cleft in the wall, then knelt down just outside the entrance with the crystal. "Move all the way back and wait."

"What are you going to do with that?" Nathaniel pointed to the rock in her hand.

"I'm going to make sure you survive what's about to happen, Nathaniel." Phoebe didn't have time to play games. "You can believe that or not. I don't care, as long as you get back there and keep Ida safe."

A screech sounded above, and a wind kicked up the dust on the floor.

"Here she comes!" Piper yelled.

"Go, Nathaniel!" Phoebe commanded. She exhaled in relief when Nathaniel vanished inside the crack in the wall.

Muffled cries and a choked scream sounded from the others when boulders moved, stalactites crashed, and the floor shook. Phoebe scanned the perimeter, but all the volunteers were still hidden. If she couldn't see them, they couldn't see her.

Paige and Piper backed off as the creature came in for a two-point landing on the ritual stone. Phoebe narrowed her eyes against the sting of swirling dust. As soon as the beast was within range, she placed the fifth crystal to activate the trap. As she had hoped, the leftover magic on the site amplified the power of the crystals, enlarging the Crystal Cage.

The Innocents were safe outside the magical prison.

The Charmed Ones were locked in with the beast.

Paige's emotions were in turmoil as she faced the fangs in the creature's slashing jaws and ducked to avoid being snagged by a hooked front claw. They had put their own and countless other lives in jeopardy when they decided to give Harriet a second chance.

But that's what we do, Paige thought. The Charmed Ones had to do everything possible to save Innocents and make sure good triumphed. If Harriet was lost because they didn't try hard enough, then Abigail's evil victory might have catastrophic consequences down the road. They simply couldn't give up while they still had a play.

"Let's do this!" Phoebe shouted as she ran up.

Paige nodded. After she and Piper had recovered from the bond with Mystic Knoll, they had decided that tapping into the ancient amplification system was too risky to attempt. Piper had forgotten the words to the spell, and she hadn't been able to talk. The unboosted Power of Three would have to be enough.

The Charmed Ones began to recite the memorized spell:

> *"Be gone cursed creature of day-night,*
> *Fang and claw invoked by spite . . ."*

The creature snarled and heaved back on its powerful hind legs. It shook its massive head, its reptilian tongue flicking toward them. Paige didn't flinch.

> *"Two times ten has now passed*
> *The child will be herself at last."*

As the last word echoed in the chamber, the beast shrieked in agony. The three sisters stood their ground when the huge winged lizard began to convulse. The tail whipped up and swung around to batter them, then suddenly went limp. Leathery wings began to shorten, the supporting ribs to recede. Yellow reptilian eyes turned brown. The cranial crest shredded into finer and finer slivers of bone, becoming hair. . . .

Paige saw Harriet's face under the translucent scales on the beast's head. She looked hopeful, determined to be free—then suddenly terrified as her face faded and another took its place. A red blotch covered the new visage's right eye.

"What's happening?" Piper shouted as the waning wind suddenly grew stronger.

"Abigail's back!" Paige pointed.

"We have to use the Mystic Knoll stones and do the spell again!" Phoebe yelled. "Now! Before she gets too strong!"

Paige knew Phoebe was right. Abigail had

made up for her lack of natural magical power with cunning. Somehow, when she died, she had transferred her essence into her newborn daughter. Her lingering spirit had easily subdued the docile Harriet within the beast, taking control to fight the power of the three witches.

"Go!" Phoebe yelled and bolted for the space between the rear and forward-right cones.

Jaws snapping and fangs bared, the beast lashed out as Phoebe dashed under a leathery wing. With Abigail in command, the monster began to regain its hideous form. Transparent scales became more opaque and hair hardened into a bony plate.

Paige hesitated, watching as Phoebe ran around the back of the raised slab and scrambled to get over the beast's useless tail. But Abigail, acting through the monster, had quickly recovered her strength. Phoebe was lifted into the air astride the tail. She jumped to the ground before she was flung into a rock wall and dashed for the magical zone between the stalagmites.

Piper attracted the beast's murderous attention as she backed up to take position between the rear and forward-left stalagmites. A prickly tongue snaked out and wrapped around Piper's leg, jerking her off her feet and pulling her away from the cones.

Paige picked up a pointed shard of stalagmite

and jabbed the beast's tongue. Roaring in pain and anger, it let Piper go, and both witches bolted for their positions.

Paige had to pinpoint the connection point. As she moved sideways in the space between the cones, she realized that the crimson crackles and pulsing red glow inside them had diminished further. She saw Phoebe stiffen an instant before the power grabbed her.

Paige fought to keep her wits and her senses functioning as she looked toward Piper. Piper's nod was almost imperceptible, but it signaled that the Charmed Ones were now part of the primal magic surging through the stones.

Paige ignored the burning within to chant the reversal spell again:

> *"Be gone cursed creature of day-night,*
> *Fang and claw invoked by spite,*
> *Two times ten has now passed*
> *The child will be herself at last."*

Her body shook so hard Paige thought her teeth would shatter in her jaws. The energies radiating from her heart into every limb were molten rivers in her veins.

Red starbursts exploded within the cones on either side of her, one after another and another. Then, as the red glow faded and the streaks fizzled out, the stalagmites crumbled.

Paige fell to her knees. Dazed and drained,

she forced herself to stay conscious. The beast was losing cohesion, and she didn't want to miss a single second of the fatal show.

A wisp of something vaguely human with a red stain fled as the creature contorted in a seizure. The last bit of Abigail had nowhere to go, nothing to cling to, and it dissipated.

The massive beast began to disintegrate, not into dust or ash, but like its creator—into nothing. The end took no more than a minute, and when the beast was gone, Harriet—wholly human and only herself—remained on the slab.

Phoebe sat on a rock and indulged in a slow exhalation of relief as everyone emerged from the underground labyrinth. The late afternoon sun streamed through the trees, drenching the ancient stone plaza in warm, golden light. Birds chirped in the trees, and a gentle breeze rustled the leaves. A sense of peace settled over everything, as though Mystic Knoll was celebrating its freedom from Abigail's malicious magic.

Phoebe exchanged a smile with Florence as she and Troy began interviewing the other witnesses. The newspaper woman and her son had questions about the events in the cavern, and she had answers. Her answers weren't factual, but they were believable.

After the beast was vanquished and before the stones had stopped rumbling, Paige covered

Harriet with the bathrobe she had stashed under a rock. She had orbed Harriet and Piper to the surface, then returned. After they retrieved the volunteers from their hiding places, Paige had enlisted Nathaniel's help to get everyone topside before another "earthquake or aftershock" brought the cavern walls down around them.

Phoebe had hung back with Ida to tell her the good news—that Harriet was alive and finally free of her mother's insidious curse. Ida had been too overjoyed to speak, but twenty years of pent-up tears had rolled down her gaunt cheeks.

Phoebe glanced across the plaza. Ida had run to her granddaughter and wrapped her arm around Harriet, as always the source of the shy young woman's comfort and support. Lucas squatted in front of his grown daughter, not saying a word, just holding her hand. Now that Abigail's spell had been broken and her spirit expelled, Harriet was cured. The monthly fits, physical manifestations of the curse, and Mystic Knoll's influence would no longer rule her life. That, plus Lucas's acceptance, was evidence that the Thornwood women wouldn't be ostracized and alone anymore.

Giggling drew Phoebe's attention to the banks of the nearby stream. Tim Barnes and Nancy Stark had taken off their shoes and socks. They were splashing in the water, getting to know each other better.

Seated on stones by the bridge, Florence was

recording as Ned talked. Piper sat with them, listening intently, making sure nobody had seen anything that exposed them.

Tammy was huddled with Gretchen, Brad, and Karen, all members of the town committee in charge of the Mystic Knoll tourist attraction. They were discussing safety concerns raised by the unexpected earthquake and cave-in. Phoebe was certain an investigation would prove the incident had been a geological fluke that would not recur.

Phoebe straightened when Paige and Nathaniel walked over. Nathaniel sat down beside her.

"Nathaniel has some questions," Paige said, "and he doesn't want to ask me."

"It's a psychology question," Nathaniel said. He hesitated, as though embarrassed. Paige took the hint and left to see how Harriet and Ida were doing. When she was out of earshot, he continued.

"I know this is going to sound ridiculous," Nathaniel said, "but I thought I saw some kind of dragon down there. Just for a second, but—"

"A dragon?" Phoebe held his troubled gaze.

"But it was Harriet." Nathaniel threw up his hands. "I know it sounds crazy—"

"Not really, Nathaniel," Phoebe said, hoping she could negate his memory and put his mind at ease. "You've been soaking up strange stories and dealing with the natural anomalies in this town for three months. I'm not at all surprised you imaged something that wasn't there, especially under these circumstances. Think about it. You were hiding in a dark cave, playing a mind trick on other people in the middle of an earthquake."

"I imagined it?" Nathaniel didn't look convinced, but he desperately wanted to be.

"Yeah." Phoebe nodded. "Or you really saw a dragon."

Nathaniel sighed, then frowned. "About that earthquake. Where did that come from?"

"Actually—" Phoebe paused, trying to come up with a plausible explanation. She had to, so Nathaniel could diffuse any speculation that circulated around town. "We were pretty sure a geological event was imminent. Old wives' tales are usually based on fact."

Nathaniel just looked at her.

"All the weird wildlife behavior," Phoebe continued. "Animals can detect changes in their surroundings, and the animals around here have been reacting to subtle hints of a major event for years."

That sounded great! Phoebe thought, keeping her fingers crossed that it sounded logical to Nathaniel.

"What does that do to the electromagnetic theory?" Nathaniel was asking himself more than her.

"That may have been a factor," Phoebe said,

"before the earthquake shifted the stones and altered the electromagnetic pattern."

Phoebe suspected that the scientific and magical forces at work in Mystic Knoll had both been changed. The stalagmite receptacles had crumbled because they couldn't withstand the Power of Three. The ancient magical amplification mechanism had been destroyed, and the animal anomalies were history.

"I think I'd better write all this down while it's still fresh in my mind. Thanks." Nathaniel rose and hurried toward his truck.

Paige immediately came back over. "Now *I* have a psychological question. More like an 'Ask Phoebe' question."

Piper overheard the last part as she strolled over to join them. "This should be good," she joked.

"I already know the answer, but in case I'm wrong . . ." Paige cleared her throat. "Nathaniel would never accept having a witch for a girlfriend, would he?"

"Nathaniel would never believe his girlfriend was a witch," Phoebe said. "Probably not a good match."

"Yeah." Paige sighed and shrugged. "That's just as well, I guess. I think Harriet has a crush on him."

"For what it's worth," Phoebe said, "the feeling may be mutual. Nathaniel just doesn't know it yet."

"Interesting," Piper said. "You won't believe

this, but most of these people are sad that the animals around town won't be going bonkers anymore."

"It is kind of sad," Phoebe said.

"Yeah, but what are the chances Harriet the beast flew all over this county without being seen?" Piper grinned. "A new local legend is born."

"At least we saved her and got rid of Abigail for good," Paige pointed out. "Ida said she was going to burn the diary."

Phoebe knew that, symbolically, destroying Abigail's spell book would help Ida and Harriet adjust and heal. The events set in motion when Ida's father had forced her to marry Joshua were finally over. The old rumors about Abigail would never die out completely, but as memories dimmed, they would lose importance.

"Can we get on with our vacation now?" Piper asked.

"Yes!" Phoebe had been so involved with Harriet and Ida's troubles she had forgotten they were supposed to be relaxing. "Are we sticking with the original plan?"

"If we were following our original schedule," Piper said, "we'd be finished touring Salem and on our way to the beach."

"If it's all right with you"—Paige looked from Piper to Phoebe—"I'd just as soon skip Salem and go directly to the beach. I've had enough New England witchcraft on this trip."

"I second that," Piper said. "Vacations shouldn't have schedules. I vote for a nice, leisurely dinner in Cairn and a fresh start in the morning."

"Good plan," Paige agreed. "I'll go ask our new friends to suggest a good restaurant."

"I'm going to duck back into the tunnels to call Leo," Piper said. "See you back at the Yankee Bear."

Before Phoebe could object, her sisters were walking away. On her own again, she walked over to Ida. She hesitated to interrupt the quiet reunion of father and daughter and stood off a couple of feet, waiting.

"What is it?" Ida asked.

"I don't know how to tell you this, Ida," Phoebe said, "but—"

"You want to stay another night," Ida finished for her.

Phoebe winced with a sheepish shrug. "Yeah."

"I've never had guests who were so hard to get rid of," Ida huffed. "One more night. No charge."

"Deal," Phoebe said. Ida's offer was an expression of gratitude for help she thought she could never repay. Phoebe couldn't explain that there was no debt without belittling the old woman's gesture.

Then Harriet smiled, and the Charmed Ones were paid in full.